Spirit Horse

NED ACKERMAN

SCHOLASTIC INC.

New York Toronto London Auckland Sydney
Mexico City New Delhi Hong Kong

ACKNOWLEDGMENTS: I want to thank Leo Pard, Blackfoot medicine man and inter-preter at Head-Smashed-In Buffalo Jump, near Fort MacLeod, Alberta, Canada, and Bob Scriver, sculptor and historian, of Browning, Montana, for their guidance. My heartfelt thanks also to Kendra Marcus, who first thought the story might be publish-able, Bernard Shir-Cliff, who believed in the story enough to try to sell it, and to Anne Dunn, my editor, who accepted that a story told from a Blackfoot point of view makes special demands. And I keep a special place in my heart for Ruth Beebe Hill, who refused to let me cheat by introducing white man's ideas into the story and showed me how to follow the moccasin path. Finally, I want to thank my family, Fran and Russell and Luke, for putting up with me while I wrote.

ISBN 0-590-39720-6

12 11 10 9 8 7 6 5   0 1 2 3/0

Printed in the U.S.A.   40

First Scholastic printing, October 1998

The text is set in 12/18 Centaur.
Cover design by Elizabeth B. Parisi
Interior design by Jessica Shatan

To my sons, Luke and Russell

May you always remember
to walk that mile
in another man's
moccasins.

Ned Ackerman was born in New Jersey and grew up in Arizona. After studying English in college, he worked as a dairy farmer and restored colonial homes. He also built and captained a 97-foot schooner, the *John F. Leavitt*, which was the last all-sail freighter in the American merchant fleet. When Mr. Ackerman decided to learn computer-assisted design, he bought a word processing program and found that he just couldn't stop writing.

Now a full-time writer, Mr. Ackerman lives in Camden, Maine, with his wife, two sons, two dogs, and (at last count) seven cats. *Spirit Horse* is his first novel for young people.

CONTENTS

CONTENTS

CHAPTER ONE

Newcomer

The horse lurched. Muscles straining, Running Crane struggled to stay on, but the ground rushed upward to slam the breath out of him.

"I told you the Siksika would fall off!" Weasel Rider shouted. He reined his plunging horse around in a tight circle, making it kick dirt onto Running Crane. "The only thing he can ride is a stump!"

The other Kainaa youths riding with Weasel Rider laughed.

"Falls Off — that should be his name."

Dizzy, but not too dizzy to burn with shame, Running Crane sucked in a deep breath, then pushed himself erect. He had fallen again, from a horse already half broken. How could he ever own a horse if he could not stay on?

Weasel Rider twisted his face into an ugly snarl. "This Siksika does not belong among Kainaa. We know horses. He knows nothing. He should *walk* back to his people in the north where he belongs."

His companions grunted their agreement.

Then Weasel Rider hooted. "The Siksika can barely ride, yet he dares talk of the spirit horse of the Snake People."

The Kainaa youths laughed again.

His store of words exhausted, Weasel Rider whipped his mount and raced away. The others followed, still laughing.

Wiping the dust from his face, Running Crane gazed wistfully at the departing riders, then at the herds dotting the prairie. The Kainaa of this new band his mother had married into owned many horses. They rode as if they had been born astride. No wonder they ridiculed him.

He yearned for a horse of his own, even a rough-gaited nag that shied at everything like this leggy bay his new stepfather let him ride. His mind drifted to the spirit horse of the Snake People — huge and fast, they said, and pale blue like the moon-of-deep-snows. The spirits watched over such a creature. If no warrior had medicine strong enough to ride the spirit horse, how could a Siksika boy newly arrived from a horse-poor band in the far north hope to? But ever since he first heard the tales, the spirit horse had thundered through his imagination.

The taunts still ringing in his ears, Running Crane set out to recapture his stepfather's bay. The horse ran to the middle of a nearby herd, then shied and dodged as horses do when they want to avoid work. The rest milled about, whickering nervously.

"Wait!" a voice called.

Running Crane looked around to see Red Calf ambling toward him, unhurried, seemingly oblivious to the herd.

Small, wiry, and tough, Red Calf had an uncanny knack with horses. "Let the horses alone until they settle down," he counseled. "Then when you go to catch the bay, do as when you hunt rabbits. Act as though you do not want the one you hunt."

When the herd returned to their grazing, Red Calf slipped among them, pretending he meant to catch a paint with a white eye. The paint trotted away and led him diagonally past the bay. Doubling back abruptly,

Red Calf caught the bay's bridle. He handed the rein to Running Crane, then caught a sorrel for himself.

"Easy for you," Running Crane said. Thoughts of the spirit horse seized his tongue. "But I shall learn. Someday I shall ride the finest. . . ." He caught himself before the rest of the words spilled out.

"Good," said Red Calf. "Now, run the bay, or you will always know fear. You say you want a fine horse of your own someday. Make yourself worthy of such a mount."

Tall for his age and lean, Running Crane swung himself onto the bay's back with ease. He urged the horse to a lope. When Red Calf raced ahead, Running Crane used the end of his rein as a quirt to whip the bay to a full run.

Holding tight to the horse's mane and gripping fiercely with his legs, he stayed on when it veered to avoid a gopher burrow. Then a grass bird flapped noisily into the air. The horse shied abruptly. Caught leaning the wrong way, Running Crane slid farther and farther off to the side. Finally, he had to release his grip and kick away or fall beneath the pounding hooves. This time he landed rolling and regained his feet quickly.

The horse slowed to a trot and started back toward

the herd, but Running Crane caught the rein and swung himself back on. He almost fell several times more, but he clung until the horse tired.

Afterward the two youths rode slowly to cool their horses, then released them into the herd.

"When will Wolf Eagle start south?" Red Calf asked.

Running Crane wished he knew. "That depends upon how far he will lead us," he said. "He has made medicine, but he keeps his counsel. The moon grows round. If we go a great distance, we will leave soon."

Red Calf grabbed his stomach and made a face. "I wish Wolf Eagle would hurry. Waiting makes me feel as if I ate a live beetle."

"I wish he would hurry, too," said Running Crane. "If he waits, he may change his mind and not take me. I wonder that he chose me this time. I am a newcomer here, and poor. Many Kainaa boys have rich fathers to speak for them. They all ride like warriors. This will be my first horse raid. You have seen *me* ride."

"Yes. But I have also seen you hunt. Wolf Eagle watched the day you stalked that pronghorn buck in the open. No four-legged one has sharper eyes than a pronghorn, yet you succeeded with only tufts of grass for cover. And I do not know how you move so quietly through the brush. Even though I am smaller than you, I make more noise."

Running Crane shrugged. "Where I lived in the north, we had few buffalo-runners. We hunted black horns on foot. Often, we hunted in the woodlands. . . ."

Memory of his father's bloody death caused Running Crane's stomach to knot. His throat tightened, and he fell silent. His father's spear had killed the black-horn bull that killed him. He died bravely, but that did not make him any less dead. Afterward, his mother had decided she must come south and marry the Kainaa husband of her older sister. Such was the custom, but Running Crane guessed she also wanted him to live in a place where warriors hunted buffalo from horseback.

"My friend remembers something," Red Calf observed quietly.

Running Crane shrugged. "I may know how to hunt, but I have no medicine."

Red Calf gasped. "No medicine?"

Running Crane shook his head.

"But you are named after the crane, the long-legged one."

"Not from a sacred dream. My father's father gave me my name after he saw a crane chase a stray dog."

Red Calf stared hard at the ground. "Perhaps you should not go."

Running Crane almost shouted, "NO!" But he caught himself. "If I stay, Wolf Eagle might never choose me again." He glanced at the distant dust plume where the other youths played horseback tag. "Weasel Rider is older than I, even older than you, and stronger, but no warrior has ever taken him on a horse raid."

If Red Calf knew why, he did not say. "Weasel Rider acts the way he does because Wolf Eagle chose you instead of him."

Not wanting to think any longer about Weasel Rider, Running Crane gazed at the herds of horses in the distance. How his Siksika friends would envy him! He closed his eyes and imagined himself riding into camp astride a mighty buffalo-runner, the finest anyone had ever seen.

The image faded, but not his determination. He missed his blood relatives, the warm feeling that came with knowing he belonged, but he would not return north.

I may fall off, he told himself. *But I shall get back on!*

CHAPTER TWO

Bad News

Running Crane enjoyed leading his stepfather's prize buffalo-runner to the river for its evening drink. He liked to watch the muscles play along the horse's withers and the alert cock of its ears. He felt the horse's strength, imagined hooves pounding as it galloped across the prairie.

Someday I shall own a horse like this one, he told himself. The wait seemed endless. He wished Wolf Eagle would —

Suddenly drums thumped in the encampment. Warriors' voices rose to fill the twilight, singing wolf songs, their songs of war.

Running Crane nearly let out a whoop. Wolf Eagle

had decided at last! The horse-raiders would leave in the morning — and he would be one of them. As soon as he staked out the buffalo-runner next to the tipi, he could take his place with the warriors as they paraded through the camp.

Sensing the excitement, the high-spirited buffalo-runner began to prance, head tossing, eyes rolling. Even though he knew he should move carefully, Running Crane tried to hurry the nervous horse. He had almost reached his stepfather's tipi when a sudden gust of wind shivered the smoke flap. The buffalo-runner shied, then reared, lashing out with its fore hooves.

Running Crane dodged clear, but the tether ripped from his grasp. Desperate not to let the horse escape, he dove headlong and caught it. Head high, the startled horse backed away, dragging the boy on his belly through the grass. He almost lost his grip, but a dog yelped, and the horse hesitated. Heaving himself to his feet, Running Crane grabbed the halter. The horse reared again, but the boy hung on.

He stroked the horse and spoke soothing words until it stood quiet, then looked around. No one would excuse his letting a valuable horse run loose in camp, a blunder far worse than merely falling off. Had anyone noticed his near disaster? No. They had gone to watch the drumming warriors and hear their songs.

Sighing his relief, Running Crane led the buffalo-runner back to his stepfather's tipi. His hands trembled, but he made every motion deliberate as he tied the knot. Then he tested it four times to make certain the tether would hold. Once he had the horse safely secured, he raced to join the warriors.

When he caught up, he almost ran into Red Calf.

"Crooked Horn has hurt his ankle," Red Calf said, his voice full of omens. "He cannot walk."

"Who goes in his place?"

Red Calf coughed and made a sour face. "Weasel Rider," he muttered, motioning with his chin toward the figure walking a few steps ahead of them.

Hearing his name, Weasel Rider turned to glare at Running Crane. "You do not belong with us, Siksika. Now that *I* am going with Wolf Eagle, my brother should also go."

Running Crane swallowed hard. "Wolf Eagle has decided," he said.

Weasel Rider sneered. "Wolf Eagle has closed his eyes. Your arms look like saplings. Your legs come from the bird of your name. You can barely ride. You talk like reeds scraping together in the wind. You dare speak of the spirit horse of the Snake People, but you know nothing about horses. You know nothing about warcraft. You have no medicine. You will bring misfortune to the raiding party. Then Wolf Eagle will see the mistake he has made."

"Wolf Eagle chose to bring Crooked Horn, Red Calf, and me," said Running Crane.

"Crooked Horn's medicine proved weak," Weasel Rider said. "But even a weakling like him would make ten of you. Wolf Eagle should leave you and take my brother."

"Speak to Wolf Eagle if you do not like his choices," Running Crane suggested.

Weasel Rider scowled. "I shall claim many victories before you learn how to stay on a dead mare. I shall capture many horses."

Running Crane could hold his own with words, if not with horses. Even though he knew his words would bring trouble later, he could not remain silent. He turned to Red Calf. "If what Weasel Rider says is so, why has no leader agreed to take such a mighty warrior on a raid until now? Why will this be his first? How many horses did his father have to pay?"

Weasel Rider's scowl darkened. "Talk while you can, Siksika. I have no need of a tongue to ride my horses for me. I shall capture many horses —"

"Enough!" Red Calf put in, although he had not begun this quarrel. "If talk could capture horses,

Weasel Rider would already own the largest herd among the Kainaa."

"Among all the Blackfoot," Running Crane added.

A trio of youths approached Wolf Eagle, each one eager to go on the raid. Fearing Wolf Eagle might choose another, Weasel Rider hastened to resume his position close behind the warrior.

Running Crane feared, too. His heart climbed into his throat every time another youth asked to go, but Wolf Eagle refused each one, saying he had the number he wanted.

After the warriors sang the last of their wolf songs, they gathered in a tight circle around Wolf Eagle so no one could overhear.

"We meet before dawn in the gully where the spring rises beside the broken cottonwood," Wolf Eagle said. "Let no one follow you."

When Running Crane returned to his tipi, he found his new stepfather, Three Belts, standing next to his buffalo-runner. Running Crane shuddered. If he had let the horse loose to run through the camp . . .

His mother, Elk Rib Woman, held open the tipi flap, then followed him inside. "Crooked Horn's injury is a bad omen," she told him in a tense whisper.

Running Crane groaned inwardly. No Blackfoot mother should urge her son to stay in camp, not even if she whispered in private.

"Wolf Eagle will lead you deep into the hunting grounds of our enemies," she warned. "You will walk for many days, perhaps a moon."

"I know how to walk," Running Crane said, remembering his days in the north. "I have done much walking."

"Perhaps you should wait until after the snows come once more," his mother said. "You would have time to learn more about horses. And you might find a warrior to share his medicine with you."

"I may not have another chance to go on a raid with Wolf Eagle," Running Crane said. "I shall learn much from him."

His mother sniffed. "Wolf Eagle has more horses than any man should have."

"More than our old band could count in our entire herd," Running Crane agreed. "Perhaps he will give horses to the youths who go with him."

"They say he has never given horses to boys. Boys go to carry warriors' moccasins and tend camp. Boys go to learn warcraft, not to gain horses for themselves." She paused, then added under her breath, "Why does Wolf Eagle take a Siksika when many Kainaa boys want to go?"

Running Crane had pondered that question many times without finding an answer. After all, he had accompanied his mother south only two moons before to live with her new husband in this Kainaa band. Their former band had owned few horses, all old and docile and easy to ride. Here he fell often, while these Kainaa youths seldom did. Yet Wolf Eagle had chosen him.

"I know only that Wolf Eagle always goes in a party of nine, six warriors and three youths," he said, too loud.

Three Belts heard. "Nine is a medicine number for Wolf Eagle," he rumbled from outside the tipi. "He has nine fingers. Long ago, ten warriors went on the raid when he won his war knife and lost his other finger. One warrior did not return. He took that as a sign. When his war party numbers the same as his fingers, all return."

"You have no medicine to protect you," his mother protested.

Embarrassed by her persistence, Running Crane turned his back. Arguing would not change her mind, or his. He waited, crossing his arms so she could not see his hands shake. When she finally left, he moved to where his sleeping skins lay on a bed of grass close beside the entrance. Kneeling, he dragged his few belongings from behind the liner that hung inside the tipi's base.

For provisions, he would take a small pouch of sun-dried buffalo meat. He wished he had some of the pemmican they prepared after the fall hunt. The nour-ishing mixture of dried buffalo meat, grease, and berries pounded together would sustain him well, but he and his mother had eaten the last of it during their trek south.

The war party would go on foot, traveling light and living off the land. Besides what he wore, he would take only a small bundle of essentials: an extra bowstring, extra moccasins, an awl, sinew to sew on new soles when they wore out, and a plain buckskin shirt such as they wore in the north, all rolled in a sleeping skin. He would carry the roll on his back with a rawhide strap across his chest.

He had made his stubby iron knife from half a longer one that had broken, and he kept the blade sharp as newly split flint. Seeing his old rabbit bow, Three Belts had given him a powerful new one, strong enough to bring down a buffalo if he aimed carefully, and a quiver of iron-tipped arrows.

Satisfied he had prepared well, Running Crane rolled his things and placed the bundle behind the tipi liner.

Using a thong tied to a lodge pole, he hung his new bow and quiver next to his old one, well off the ground to prevent damage from any dampness. Then he went for a long walk to consider his mother's warnings.

He had no medicine of his own. No kindly spirit had come to him in a dream and offered protection. No warrior had taught him a wolf song. The wolf songs reminded him of how unprotected and vulnerable he would be without strong medicine.

His heart began to sink, but he heard a horse whinny. That reminded him why he wanted to go on the raid. He wanted horses of his own. For even a single horse, he would suffer Weasel Rider's company.

CHAPTER THREE

Seeds of Fear

If Running Crane kept his eyes shut for the space of ten breaths during the night, he could not remember. Unable to sleep, he rose long before the appointed time, pulled his roll from behind the tipi liner, then groped for his new bow. Something brushed the back of his hand — the thong he had used, hanging free.

He crawled under the liner to search. His old bow and arrows, which he still kept for small game, hung in their usual place. They hung alone. A slack area in the tipi cover sagged where a peg had worked loose. He found nothing else.

His mother did not want him to go. Could she have hidden his new bow? An unthinkable thing for a Blackfoot mother to do, but . . . He could not waken the others to ask. They would laugh at him, and one of his older stepbrothers might try to follow, and then Wolf Eagle *would* leave him behind.

Three Belts rolled onto his side and groaned, his breathing uneasy. In desperation, Running Crane slung his gear on his back, caught up his old bow and arrows, and crept out.

The moon, nearly full, hung almost overhead, and the Last Brother still pointed up, toward the west. He had started early, but once on his way he did not stop. Four times he doubled back on his trail and watched from cover to make certain no one followed, but still he reached the broken cottonwood long before the others.

Alone in the dark, the thumping of his heart his only company, he pondered whether Wolf Eagle would come. Had the warrior changed his mind and secretly told the others to meet in a different place? After what seemed forever, the Seven Brothers swung low in the sky, pivoting around the star-that-never-moves, and the moon sank. The appointed time approached.

Then grass hissed against a legging, and pebbles crunched softly beneath a moccasin. Man-shaped shadows emerged one by one from the darkness until they numbered nine. Including Running Crane, that made ten. Chill apprehension crawled up his spine. Would Wolf Eagle leave him behind after all?

The last pair had arrived together — an interloper had followed in hopes Wolf Eagle would accept him. A shadow moved toward them. When Wolf Eagle's voice grated like a flint blade scraping on a rock, the larger of the two latecomers backed away.

Without another word, Wolf Eagle set off.

The experienced warriors fanned out ahead on both sides to scout, even though they traveled their own hunting grounds. No great danger threatened here, but if Blackfoot could raid for horses, so could Crow People and Snake People. The three boys walked in silence near the center of the formation.

Running Crane knew they would go south and west, but not what path they would take. In the short time he had lived among the Kainaa, he had only barely begun to explore these new hunting grounds, but he knew how to travel in the night. He could hear the footsteps of a warrior ahead and to the right. Now and again as they crossed a roll in the land, he glimpsed a shadow moving against the stars, all he needed to keep up.

Dawn brightened pale rose and gray. By the time Running Crane could distinguish the features of the warriors farther away, their encampment lay invisible in a hilly sea of waving grass that stretched unbroken to the horizon. Only the ancient buffalo trails, worn deep into the sod where the immense, black-horned ground-walkers had followed the same path for untold generations, marked the vastness.

Long-eared rabbits bounded away, running a hundred paces or so, then stopping to stare at the intruders. Others remained motionless as stones, hoping to remain unseen until the humans passed. Overhead a blunt-winged hawk circled lazily in search of an unwary mouse or prairie dog.

The war party halted in a swale while Hunts-Smoke-Rising kept watch from a nearby rise. A peerless scout, Hunts-Smoke-Rising almost never spoke. No enemy would catch the war party unaware as long as he kept a lookout for danger.

Boys accompanied raiding parties to carry the warriors' gear. Now the warriors transferred what part of their loads they wished. Beaver-Slaps-Tail-Twice brought only spare moccasins for the boys to carry. Otter carried enough for three men. Youngest of the warriors and usually cheerful, he acted deadly serious now they had taken the war trail. He transferred a large part of his load to Weasel Rider.

Owl Child, oldest of the warriors, handed his extra

moccasins to Running Crane. Although a famed taker of horses and known to possess very strong medicine, Owl Child preferred to have Wolf Eagle lead. Small Dog, whose name belied his great size, strength, and appetite, delivered a large pouch of dried meat to Red Calf. He had another, and he turned his huge head toward Running Crane, then toward Weasel Rider, then back before he decided his extra provisions might last longer with Running Crane. Wolf Eagle had divided his spares into three parcels. He handed one to each boy, giving Running Crane two strong buffalo-hide ropes to carry.

The warriors set out again before Running Crane could settle his new burden into place. They paused only to drink from the small creeks that meandered across their path. Below the crest of every ridge, they scanned the prairie for signs of enemies before exposing themselves to view. Running Crane spent a good while shifting his load this way and that so the strap would not chafe his shoulder. Once he arranged his burden comfortably, he realized he felt hungry. In his turmoil about the missing bow, he had neglected to eat.

Days of the moon-when-grass-becomes-green grow long, but this one seemed to go on forever. Running

Crane's excitement about their departure faded, replaced by the gnawing emptiness in his stomach. He thought about his small supply of dried meat, but he might need that in an emergency. He decided his stomach could wait.

Late in the afternoon, he strung his old bow, drew a blunt arrow from his quiver, and began watching for a jackrabbit which might have frozen in place behind a clump of grass. When he saw one, he took care not to look directly at it. He maintained a course that would apparently carry him a safe distance past the hiding creature. Suddenly he pushed his bow and loosed the arrow. Hit squarely, the rabbit made one prodigious leap, screamed, then lay jerking until Running Crane snapped its neck. He gutted the carcass quickly and hurried to catch the others.

Red Calf ignored the rabbit. Instead he talked about horses. "I have wondered why you are not a rider even though you vault easily onto a horse's back."

"My father owned few horses," Running Crane explained. "When we moved our camp, one horse dragged the travois loaded with our lodge cover. My mother rode that one. We tied up our lodge poles and camp goods for two other horses to drag. My older sisters rode those two or walked beside them if the loads became too heavy. My father rode the last horse. I walked."

"But did you not learn to ride when you made camp?"

"Our horses were old. A baby could ride any one of them," Running Crane said. He looked down at his long legs and grinned crookedly. "But I could always practice getting on."

Red Calf grinned, too.

"Even walking," Running Crane said, "life was good until a buffalo killed my father. . . . " His voice trailed away.

Sensing his friend's sadness, Red Calf fell silent.

They made camp in a hollow that guarded a trickle of sweet water. The boys gathered sun-bleached sticks and dried buffalo chips while Owl Child kindled a small cooking fire. He built it beneath a tree so the leafy crown would break up the wisps of rising smoke.

Hunts-Smoke-Rising appeared, seemingly from nowhere. He threw a slice of buffalo meat onto the fire. The fat sizzled and spat until he plucked his supper from the flames and departed as silently as he had come.

Running Crane skinned his kill, then spitted the carcass on a green branch. He waited until the others had finished cooking before he set the meat to roast over the coals.

Weasel Rider had brought a packet heavy with strips of smoke-cured buffalo meat. Eating with noisy relish, he glowered at Running Crane. "No true Blackfoot eats rabbit," he announced, his voice filled with scorn. "Snake People eat rabbit. A true Blackfoot eats real meat — buffalo."

Running Crane tended the fire and turned the branch so the meat would cook evenly.

"Is that all Siksikas eat — rabbit?" Weasel Rider asked.

Running Crane did not answer. He hunkered on the opposite side of the fire and gazed steadfastly at his rabbit. His stomach churned, but this time not from hunger. The warriors would not interfere unless Weasel Rider's persecutions threatened the success of their raid. This was boys' business, not men's.

Weasel Rider sneered. "You eat fish, too." Despite the abundance of trout in the streams, the Blackfoot considered fish unclean. Weasel Rider went on to name other foods a Blackfoot would not eat. "And snakes and lizards and grizzly meat — if you find one long enough dead and rotting."

Running Crane retrieved his rabbit from the coals, then bit off a mouthful and chewed deliberately.

"Maybe you are Cree," Weasel Rider said. "Maybe you eat dogs and skunks and badgers."

Running Crane pretended not to hear. He continued chewing and tried to let no expression cross his face which might give Weasel Rider more cause for his torments.

Weasel Rider grew angry when Running Crane refused to respond. He stalked around the fire and kicked sand on the rabbit.

"Sssst!" came Beaver-Slaps-Tail-Twice's hiss from the darkness, barely audible, yet sharply penetrating.

Weasel Rider fumbled for words, his eyes glowing with hatred. Unable to muster a final, telling insult, he shoved Running Crane backward. Running Crane went down hard. Weasel Rider stood over him glaring, and Running Crane braced for another attack.

"Sssst!" Beaver-Slaps-Tail-Twice repeated, demanding silence.

Weasel Rider hesitated, then spun away and stalked into the darkness.

Safe for the moment, Running Crane rolled to his feet and brushed himself off as if he had tripped by accident. Scraping the sand off his meat, he rinsed it in the spring and began to eat. He chewed until the bones gleamed, although he no longer felt hungry. The rabbit tasted dry and bitter now, but he would need his strength.

Doubts gnawed at him. Weasel Rider had not called him "Falls Off" within hearing of the warriors, but did they know how often he fell? Would they send him back if they learned that he had no medicine? He could not silence Weasel Rider, and if he did not have medicine strong enough to protect himself from the older youth, what would happen when they found real enemies?

CHAPTER FOUR

The Trail South

The next morning, Weasel Rider dropped the leather hobbles Wolf Eagle had given him onto Running Crane's sleeping skin and then strode haughtily away. Running Crane lashed the hobbles to Wolf Eagle's ropes and carried the added burden without complaint. The following day, Weasel Rider left behind part of what Otter had given him. Running Crane carried that, too.

Now the endless walking he had done in the north served him well. Despite his leanness, he had carried many heavy burdens over long distances. His stride never faltered.

In camp, Weasel Rider acted as if he had already earned the status of a seasoned warrior, leaving his share of fetching wood and tending the fire for Running Crane. If the men noticed, they gave no sign. Running Crane endured the impositions in silence. He killed small game as he walked and roasted the meat at night while Weasel Rider chewed on his dried buffalo and attempted to look superior.

They met herd after herd of buffalo making their unhurried way northward, following the bunchgrass in their yearly migration, always eating. First one would appear, then a group. Soon a dark flood of the grazing brown creatures would cover the prairie.

Occasional herds of large-eyed pronghorns, always alert for danger, stared curiously at the passing humans. At the slightest threat, they bounded away, their hindquarters bobbing white against the green grass. Elk and deer browsed on the tender shoots of brush and trees along the creek beds that meandered across the prairie.

Not all the prairie dwellers ate grasses or green shoots. Packs of wolves lurked along the flanks of the vast buffalo herds, hunting for a straggling calf or an adult too injured or too old to escape. In the hours of darkness, their eerie howls echoed back and forth across the plains. Overhead, sharp-eyed hawks and broad-winged eagles soared high on the winds, and buzzards circled lazily in search of the dead or dying.

Once, a huge silver-tipped grizzly down from the mountains wandered across their path. It followed their trail until they made camp, then prowled downwind, sniffing their scent and grunting.

In addition to their enormous strength, grizzlies possessed enormous spiritual power. Their weapons ready for instant use, the warriors held a taut-voiced council and debated whether this one might be a medicine bear.

Owl Child brought forth a small feathered charm which he set before him. He burned a tuft of sweet grass on a glowing coal and sang a medicine song. After a time, the grizzly lumbered off, and Owl Child put his charm away.

Impressed by the strength of Owl Child's medicine, Running Crane wished again that he had some medicine of his own.

One day when the sun had just begun to sink, Wolf Eagle called a halt in a sheltered valley. Soon they would enter the hunting grounds of their enemies. Once there, they would not cook because the wind could carry the aromas of smoke and roasting meat a great distance. Now they needed fresh meat to last them until they made a permanent camp.

Hunts-Smoke-Rising, who had appeared and disappeared at irregular intervals since their trek began, returned from his scouting to announce that a herd of buffalo grazed in a watered bottom nearby. He whispered something to Beaver-Slaps-Tail-Twice before he slipped away again. Beaver-Slaps-Tail-Twice frowned thoughtfully.

The warriors consulted their medicine and inspected their bows, giving special attention to their twisted-sinew bowstrings.

Red Calf and Weasel Rider each had fine, recurved bows made of chokecherry backed with buffalo sinew. Running Crane had made his old bow of chokecherry, too, but he had used thinner sinew backing. Although he could trust the bow only for small game, he might succeed in killing a very young calf with a perfectly placed arrow. The bow had grown far too limber to drive an arrow a killing distance into a full-grown buffalo.

Weasel Rider smirked knowingly. "Something happened to the new bow Three Belts gave Running Crane," he said to Red Calf. "Running Crane does not command medicine strong enough to keep a powerful bow. Perhaps the bow feared he would drop it and run away. Perhaps the bow lifted the skirt of his tipi and escaped while he slept." With that, Weasel Rider walked away laughing.

Red Calf made a face as if he had found half a caterpillar wriggling in his sarvice berries. "Weasel Rider stole your bow."

"Why?" Running Crane wondered aloud.

"Perhaps he thought you would stay with the band if you could not find it. You saw the other one who came with him, the one Wolf Eagle sent away? That was Weasel Rider's half-brother, Black Cloud. Black Cloud is younger, but bigger and ill-tempered. He hurt Crooked Horn because he expected Wolf Eagle to choose him in Crooked Horn's place. Their father gave Wolf Eagle four horses to take Weasel Rider instead. Weasel Rider fears Black Cloud. When Black Cloud bullies Weasel Rider, Weasel Rider finds someone else to bully."

"We have walked together many days," said Running Crane, "yet you did not tell me this until now."

Red Calf spoke slowly, grimacing as if his words tasted like ashes. "I do not like Weasel Rider, but I did not want to believe he would do so dishonorable a thing. Now he has said too much. Watch your back.

If he cannot drive you away with words, he will try deeds."

"I could not go back, whatever Weasel Rider does," said Running Crane. "No medicine dream has come to warn me away. I shall go on. To do otherwise would be cowardly."

Red Calf glanced at Weasel Rider. "If Weasel Rider forced such an act upon you, his boast of it would go far to soothe Black Cloud's anger."

Wolf Eagle called the party together. "Buffalo graze beyond the second ridge," he said. "The wind blows from the west. The warriors shall go toward the east so the black horns do not catch our scent. The boys shall circle to the west and move the herd toward us. Take care not to make the buffalo run. Our enemies might see their dust and wonder what startled them."

He drove a stick in the ground and made a mark two handbreadths east of the tip of its shadow. "You shall move when the shadow touches the mark," he told the boys.

The warriors started off with Hunts-Smoke-Rising in the lead. Beaver-Slaps-Tail-Twice went last. Without pausing as he passed the three boys, he warned quietly, "Beware the bull!"

While the shadow crept toward the mark, Running

Crane sat by himself and pondered the hunt. He had driven black horns many times, and hunting on foot always scared him. Then a black-horn bull had killed his father. Memory of his father's bloody death caused Running Crane's stomach to knot. Still, his father had known the risks, and he had accepted them cheerfully.

Recalling his father's fearlessness enabled Running Crane to dry his sweating hands upon the grass and stand. He would do no less than his father had done. He tucked his buckskin shirt into the back of his waist-band and strung his bow.

All the while Running Crane sat gathering his courage, Weasel Rider boasted about all the buffalo he had killed and about how he would kill a buffalo today if the warriors failed. The instant the shadow brushed the mark, he started running, as if he could ensure his success with speed instead of stealth. When Running Crane and Red Calf bent low to cross the second ridge, they saw Weasel Rider well out on the treeless bottom, still moving fast. Several buffalo had raised their heads to peer in his direction.

The ridge ran to the east and sloped gently downward. On the far side of the bottom, a creek flowed. Willows grew in dense clumps by the water's edge and filled the air with their pungent scent. In its perpetual meanderings across the grassy flat, the creek had abandoned many old channels, leaving narrow trenches, several chest-deep.

Beyond the creek rose a nearly vertical cut bank which curved sharply where an area of harder soil resisted the scouring action of the flowing water. At its end, the creek fanned out into a braid of smaller flows, and a scattering of willows grew on little islands between them. There the warriors would wait in ambush.

The herd numbered fewer than two hundred. Most of the cows had calves. Some lay placidly chewing their cuds; others grazed. A flock of birds foraged under their noses, hunting the insects they stirred up. Once disturbed, the buffalo would either follow the water course downstream toward the willows, or they would come up the slope. Or, they might simply decide to charge.

From high on the ridge, the feeding creatures appeared small and docile, but Running Crane knew these prairie buffalo were neither. True, they did not grow as large as the buffalo who roamed the wooded uplands where he used to live. But a big one stood taller than a man at the shoulder and weighed twice as much as a horse.

One huge bull grazing on the far side of the herd stood taller than the rest. "His singular yellowish color might mark him as a bull the spirits noticed," Running Crane thought, "a bull of great power." Killing such an animal would bring strong medicine. He tested his bow, then abandoned the idea. No matter how accurate his aim, his bow lacked the strength to bring down a full-grown buffalo, and he felt relief the bull grazed no closer.

"Take the slope," he told Red Calf. "If they bolt this way, you may kill one."

Red Calf grinned and shook his bow. Moving another twenty steps down the slope, he started working his way along a buffalo trail that paralleled the crest. Running Crane could not grin when he moved onto the flat; too much could go wrong.

CHAPTER FIVE

The Hunt
and the Hunted

Once Running Crane reached the grassy bottom, the black horns looked big and dangerous. Three or four stood and faced toward him. Not keen of vision like pronghorns, they peered shortsightedly around, grunting to one another and waiting for the danger to reveal itself.

As he gazed at the buffalo, Running Crane's heart thumped like a medicine drum, and the bitter taste of fear filled his mouth. Was this how his father had felt before the black horn bull killed him? His father had gone on anyway.

Running Crane jumped two of the old channel cuts and walked slowly toward the buffalo. The bottom offered no place to hide if they charged. His safety lay in confusing the black horns and heading them in the other direction. With Weasel Rider helping, they could move them easily. But Weasel Rider had gotten so far ahead that he might start the herd the wrong way. When Weasel Rider dodged into the willows, Running Crane relaxed just a little.

He pulled the shirt from his waistband and draped it over the tip of his bow. Extending the bow high over his head, he waved the shirt slowly from side to side. More buffalo lurched to their feet. The herd could smell and see him now. They knew where their enemy stood, but not what danger threatened.

He summoned his courage and stepped slowly toward them.

The nearest cow decided she could find better grass elsewhere and ambled away. Another cow followed, and another. Up on the ridge, Red Calf also began to wave. A young bull backed away, not really afraid, but wary. On the far side of the herd, several grazers retreated without waiting to learn more about the threat. The buffalo began moving, not hurrying, but moving.

Left behind by its mother, a young calf bawled in

alarm. The cow bawled, too. Three young bulls moved to guard the cow and calf as if they expected wolves. A note of alarm spread through the herd, and a few young cows broke into a trot. One strayed near the willows by the edge of the creek where Weasel Rider hid. As the cow passed the tawny bull, she spun suddenly around, bawling at the top of her lungs. An arrow stuck from her haunch. Unable to wait, Weasel Rider sent another arrow at the tawny bull and missed, then retreated into the willows.

With danger on both sides, the buffalo milled about grunting as they sought their tormentors. Running Crane lowered his shirt and froze in his tracks. The moving buffalo would have difficulty seeing him as long as he did not stir.

Suddenly the tawny bull left the others and started trotting deliberately in Running Crane's direction. With a high hump and a beard that brushed the ground, the bull looked like a four-legged mountain. His curved, black horns had grown so long the tips pointed toward each other.

"Perhaps he *is* a spirit bull," thought Running Crane. "Perhaps that is why Weasel Rider missed after he crept close."

The bull lifted his nose high to sniff the wind, then

pawed the earth. Closer and closer he came, turning his shaggy head from side to side and rolling his beady eyes, searching. He spied Running Crane and lumbered to a stop.

Even though he knew he should stand still, Running Crane dropped his shirt and stepped slowly backward. Visions of his father's mangled body whirled before his eyes. The bull bellowed, and Running Crane's nerve broke. He had nowhere to run, but he ran. The bull charged after him.

Running Crane could run as fast as anyone he knew, but the bull ran much faster. He caught Running Crane easily. Running Crane dodged, barely escaping a swipe of the horns, and the bull thundered past. The bull skidded to a halt. Pivoting with agility amazing for such a huge creature, he bellowed and charged again. Running Crane stood his ground until the last instant, then threw himself to the side and started to run. The bull wheeled and caught him again. Again he dodged, barely evading those hooking horns.

Running Crane jumped a dry channel in hopes the bull would stop. The bull soared effortlessly across. Running Crane tripped. He rolled instantly to his feet, but the bull pivoted again, one horn aimed at the center of his gut. Running Crane twisted away. The horn's outer curve grazed his side and knocked him down. Running Crane rolled desperately.

Suddenly, the earth seemed to open up and swallow him. He landed flat on his back in a dry channel. He heard the bull's enraged bellows, then swirling darkness sucked him down.

CHAPTER SIX

Dead or Alive?

Running Crane could hear Red Calf call his name, but his eyes refused to open. He tried to move, but he could not. Did dying always feel this way, being able to hear but not see or move? Would he walk the Wolf Trail now to join his father at the Sand Hills of the dead?

He tried to shout, but earth filled his mouth. More earth held him down. He struggled to free an arm and push the soil from his face. By the time he got his eyes open, Red Calf loomed above him, silhouetted against the sky.

"Ho," called Red Calf, looking down. "I did not

know a buffalo covered his kill the way a grizzly does. He has left you here to season before he returns to eat you."

He laughed at his joke and dropped lightly into the dry channel to help his friend dig out. They recovered Running Crane's bow. His quiver still hung at his back, but they could not find his shirt.

"Tell me what happened," Running Crane demanded.

"You disappeared," said Red Calf. "The bull could not find you. He stood on the edge looking for you, and the bank collapsed. He fell in. Then he jumped around as if you were trying to trap him from a pit the way a warrior traps an eagle. You would have laughed to see him."

Running Crane did not feel like laughing. He spat and stretched to make sure all his parts still worked. Then he looked where he had fallen. Buffalo tracks covered every handbreadth of the ground except that one spot. He made washing motions and staggered toward the creek, shaking his head in numbed disbelief.

Clean but still dripping, he hurried to the turn in the cutbank where the warriors had lain in wait. They had killed two young cows. Small Dog and Otter had begun butchering one. Working on the other, Owl Child motioned Running Crane to help him.

Running Crane's side ached, but he did not pity himself. In fact, he felt as if he could fly. He still lived after he had been so certain he would die. Some spirit had spared him, even if he did not know which one. Perhaps he would have a medicine dream now and the spirit would reveal itself. His joy made the butchering effortless, and he smiled as he worked.

Owl Child removed the liver and offered Running Crane a thick slice. Running Crane ate the liver raw, as hunters often did when they killed.

"Just take meat," Owl Child instructed. They would not do the heavy butchering of a community hunt when the hunters quartered their kills and carried them back to camp. "Take no hide. Do not cut the joints apart. Leave no knife marks on the bones to let our enemies know men have fed from these black horns. We will give what we do not take to the sun. Wolves will feast on what the sun does not want, but wolves do not carry knives. After the wolves, coyotes will come, and ravens. Soon the carcasses will seem as if wolves had made the kills."

Eating more raw liver as he worked, Running Crane stripped off the meat and set it out to dry, leaving the bones intact. By the time he finished, he was so full he could hardly move.

Owl Child grunted his approval. "You know how to butcher, Siksika."

Weasel Rider did not appear until they completed the butchering.

Wolf Eagle decided to wait another day to dry their meat, then set out the next night. Running Crane slept poorly. The bull charged through his dreams, and his side ached where the horn had grazed him. He awoke panting several times, his body shaking and slick with fear-sweat. To his great disappointment, the spirit who had aided him remained invisible.

After breakfasting on buffalo meat, he went to search again for the shirt he had lost. When he could not find it, he returned to camp and sharpened his knife, which the butchering had dulled. Miraculously, his bow had escaped undamaged, but he had smashed three of his arrows when he fell. He removed their points and carved off the feathers, then buried the broken shafts where they would not be found. The fall had bent several other arrows. These he carefully straightened before he joined Red Calf in the shade of a cottonwood.

"I thought the bull had killed you," Red Calf said.

"So did I," Running Crane agreed.

Red Calf gazed into the distance, then twisted a

blade of grass between his fingers. "You have strong medicine."

Running Crane shrugged. "You saw what happened. I fell. The bank collapsed. The sod protected me. I do not know why. No dream came to tell me what to do."

"I see more than that." Red Calf sounded certain.

"Falls Off has no medicine," Weasel Rider put in. Walking to the cottonwood, he stood over Running Crane and glared. "He almost caused our hunt to fail. He should leave us before he brings more misfortune."

"Weasel Rider does not understand what happened," Running Crane said to Red Calf. "Perhaps the willows blocked his view."

"Falls Off can do nothing useful except butcher our kills," Weasel Rider persisted. "Maybe he belongs with the old women."

Running Crane's patience ran out. After his narrow escape, Weasel Rider did not seem so fearsome. "Weasel Rider seems unable to do his share around the camp," he told Red Calf in disgust. "He did no butchering. I doubt that he could live without his mother to build his fires and chew his meat."

Weasel Rider roared at the suggestion and leaped upon Running Crane, shouting insults. Unable to defend himself against the sudden attack by the larger boy, Running Crane curled into a tight ball and waited it out. Weasel Rider soon exhausted himself, but not before inflicting many painful bruises.

"Stand up, Siksika coward," Weasel Rider hissed. When Running Crane did not, Weasel Rider kicked sand on him and stamped away.

Running Crane uncurled, stifling a groan. *Red Calf has spoken the truth*, he thought. *Weasel Rider will not stop.* Pondering the things Weasel Rider might do in the dark made him shiver.

When the sun dipped behind the distant mountains, which the Blackfoot called Backbone-of-the-World, Beaver-Slaps-Tail-Twice gathered the boys together. Hunts-Smoke-Rising stood with him.

"Tonight we enter the hunting grounds of our enemies," said Beaver-Slaps-Tail-Twice. "We must leave no trace of our passing. If you send an arrow, recover the arrow wherever it falls." He withdrew two arrows from his quiver, one bloodied, one clean, and handed them to Weasel Rider. "Even from the flank of a buffalo."

The arrows proved both Weasel Rider's carelessness and his poor aim, but he glared as if to blame Running Crane for his failure.

"If you lose an article of clothing," Beaver-Slaps-Tail-Twice continued, "recover that, too. Leave no sign that we have passed this way."

Hunts-Smoke-Rising brought forth a tattered bundle which he handed to Running Crane: his buckskin shirt, trampled by buffalo hooves.

"Be glad you took this off before the spirit bull found it," Beaver-Slaps-Tail-Twice added with a solemn wink.

Hunts-Smoke-Rising nodded in grave agreement.

Running Crane did not know what to say. These warriors had carefully cleaned the shirt of sand and grass. They had given him a harsh warning, but they also showed they approved what he had done. Suddenly his bruises ached less.

"From here on," said Wolf Eagle, looking sternly at the boys, "all games cease."

Traveling during the starlit night felt little different from traveling in the daylight. The party kept the same order, the warriors fanned out ahead, boys in the center. They took the same precautions crossing the tops of ridges. They avoided stepping in the dust of the old, deeply-worn buffalo trails where they would leave moccasin prints. Sleeping during the day proved the hardest part.

Watching the others consult their medicine and listening as they sang appeals to the spirits for safety and success, Running Crane felt empty because he had no medicine himself, no songs to sing. He thanked the sun for his escape from the tawny bull, but he wished fervently for a sacred dream. When no dream came to him, his fear grew. Every step he took seemed heavier than the one before.

A range of hills rose on the horizon to the southwest. By dawn of the fourth day, the hills stretched far across their path, and Running Crane knew they would reach the wooded ridges the next night. Somewhere on the other side of those hills, they would find a camp of their enemies and the horses they had come to take.

The very thought of horses lifted the weight from his feet, and he grew impatient.

CHAPTER SEVEN

The War Lodge

The hills formed a narrow spur extending eastward from Backbone-of-the-World. Thick stands of lodge-pole pines covered the slopes. Scattered among them grew clumps of pale-barked aspens whose leaves shivered at the slightest breeze.

Running Crane liked moving among the trees. Pine needles underfoot silenced his steps. Their fragrance soothed him, and the wind whistling softly through the boughs brought memories of his former home.

An enemy could not see the war party from any great distance here, but jays flew from branch to branch ahead of them, calling noisily. Knowing an enemy scout might notice the disturbance, Wolf Eagle called a halt. They ate and rested quietly until dark, then pushed on.

Even with the terrain broken and confusing, Wolf Eagle knew his path. He led the way across the spine of the foothills and followed a ridge southward. After a thin sliver of the old moon rose low in the eastern sky, he stopped on a knoll surrounded by dense woods.

Hunts-Smoke-Rising arrived silently. He did no more than salute Wolf Eagle before he disappeared among the trees. Wolf Eagle dropped his pack and stretched, then plunged into a blowdown of lodgepole pines. Finding a sheltered site overlooking a steep, open slope, he used his knife to chop the small branches off a fallen tree. The others did the same.

Within minutes, they raised a rough frame for their war lodge — conical, like a buffalo-hide tipi, and just large enough for all to sleep inside. They covered the poles with branches and bark, leaving a smoke hole at the top. To fortify the lodge, they piled the heaviest logs they could move around the base. They also built a long, angled entrance with more thick timbers. That way, no enemy could see the light of their fire from the outside, and no arrow could fly directly in. With the entire party working together, they completed the war lodge by sunrise.

After helping Small Dog heave the last log in place, Running Crane brushed off the bits of bark that clung to him and looked around. Nearby, a bold outcropping of rock topped by a single wind-blasted pine provided a view of the grasslands below. But no enemy could see the site Wolf Eagle had chosen from the prairie.

At the base of the hill, a small, willow-choked creek followed a winding course onto the prairie. Because dry willow burned almost without smoke, Beaver-Slaps-Tail-Twice sent Running Crane and Red Calf to the creek for wood. By the time they returned, the others had spread their robes inside the lodge and fallen asleep, all except Hunts-Smoke-Rising and Owl Child. Wolf Eagle had sent them to scout for an enemy camp.

Two experienced men could remain concealed more easily than the entire party. They had taken wolf skins to wear as disguises while they searched for signs. First they would examine the country from the high places, alert for any sudden movements of birds or ground-walkers that might be fleeing humans. They would examine trails for telltale tracks. They would search for sites where the enemy might set up camp while they hunted buffalo, and they would sniff the air for the smells of cooking. If they found a camp, they would scout to determine the number of warriors and horses.

And they would take great care not to give themselves away.

Running Crane could find only a narrow space beside the entrance for his sleeping skin, with the bulk of Small Dog between him and the fire. Exhausted after the night's climb through the hills and raising the lodge, he tried to sleep, but sleep would not come. Going on a raid had seemed simple before, hardly more than a long walk with a herd of horses waiting and a mount to ride home. With Weasel Rider constantly hostile, he had given little thought to the enemy. Building the war lodge reminded him of the danger. Although they came to take horses, not scalps, their enemies would fight and kill if they could.

Hunts-Smoke-Rising and Owl Child did not return that day or the next. Those left at the war lodge hunted in the hills to secure food for their homeward journey. Otter killed a fat elk. Soon many strips of meat hung drying around their lodge.

Running Crane had worn the bottoms of both pairs of moccasins dangerously thin. He decided to sew on new elkhide soles.

"Running Crane can only do the work of women," Weasel Rider jeered.

Running Crane pretended he did not hear and kept

on sewing. Weasel Rider made him feel angry now, instead of embarrassed, but he said nothing. The time to settle with Weasel Rider had not come yet, but suddenly he knew that the time *would* come, and dark apprehension chilled him.

Shortly after midday, puffy clouds piled higher and higher over the mountains. Thunder walked, stabbing jagged lightning at the peaks. Otter and Small Dog held a private council, then sent the boys for more wood. When Weasel Rider made to refuse, Small Dog growled at him, a threat Weasel Rider understood. He left the war lodge with Running Crane and Red Calf, but he deserted as soon as Small Dog could no longer see him. He remained absent when the two returned.

Small Dog and Otter glanced at the sky and fussed about the lodge cover. Thunder's rumbling grew louder, and lightning bolts cast hard-edged shadows on the ground. The storm broke with a cold gust of wind and small hail pellets rattling through the pines. Weasel Rider appeared. He ducked into the war lodge and retired to his sleeping robe. Small Dog and Otter followed. Moments later a blast of wind whipped the trees, and rain roared down loud enough to drown out all but the loudest thunder.

Safe under cover, Running Crane lay back and

listened as the warriors discussed the meaning of the storm.

"Our journey has gone well," declared Wolf Eagle. "Our medicine grows strong. The storm hides our tracks."

The other warriors agreed.

Small Dog and Otter were sharing a private joke. A series of covert grins passed between them, and they kept sneaking glances at Weasel Rider. Running Crane peeked at Weasel Rider, too, hoping to discover what they expected, but Weasel Rider saw his gaze and scowled darkly. Running Crane looked quickly away. Suddenly Weasel Rider yelped and leaped to his feet, clutching his sleeping robe. Where his bed had lain, a cascade of rain water gushed from the lodge cover.

"Ho," Small Dog told Otter loudly. "Such is the fate of one who neglects his share of work in camp."

"Weasel Rider's rain medicine grows strong," Otter chimed in. "Perhaps he should have given more help when we covered the lodge."

Beaver-Slaps-Tail-Twice laughed until he gasped for air. Aloof and silent, Wolf Eagle rubbed the stump of his missing finger, but a gleam in his eye showed he felt satisfied. A leak deliberately left in a lodge cover was a common way of punishing an indolent member of a war party. The tension broken, laughs and derisive comments continued as the warriors assured themselves that Weasel Rider had paid well for his laziness. Someone even suggested he might seize the opportunity to bathe.

A wave of relief washed through Running Crane. Even though the warriors had not meddled in the affairs of the boys, they had overlooked neither Weasel Rider's arrogance nor his slothfulness. Knowing that made him feel better.

Weasel Rider shook the water from his robe, but he had to remain standing. He saw no other space in the lodge big enough for him to lie down, and no one offered to make room.

Running Crane tried to remain expressionless, but a triumphant grin possessed his face when he realized Weasel Rider thought he had contrived the hole. Now he felt happy to have Small Dog sleeping between himself and Weasel Rider, even if the warrior's bulk did block the fire's warmth.

As abruptly as it began, the squall ended, leaving the forest dripping noisily. The sun emerged from behind the departing clouds to warm the air, and pale tendrils of evaporating mist rose wherever the light touched.

Weasel Rider spread his robe outside the war lodge to

dry and squatted sullenly next to it, daring Running Crane or Red Calf to snicker. His baleful glare followed Running Crane's every movement about the camp.

Once he managed to control his laughter, Running Crane began to ponder what Weasel Rider might do in revenge. He decided to carry his bow and arrows at all times. When Weasel Rider grudgingly left camp on an errand for Otter, Running Crane gathered up his extra pair of newly repaired moccasins, his dried meat, and the other small odds and ends from his pack. Then he stole well back into the woods to find them a safe hiding place.

The sky over the mountains soon became pale and milky, and thin streamers of cloudlike horsetails blowing in the wind reached high over the prairie. The fierce squall had not lasted, but it foretold a change in the weather. Running Crane wondered what else would change.

No sooner had he returned to the war lodge than everyone rushed to the edge of the slope. Running Crane hurried to join them.

Looking downward, he saw Hunts-Smoke-Rising and Owl Child, still wearing their wolfskin disguises, zigzagging toward the lodge. The zigzagging meant success. They had found the enemy!

CHAPTER EIGHT

A Mysterious Prophecy

When Wolf Eagle saw Hunts-Smoke-Rising and Owl Child zigzagging up the slope, he strode down to greet them. The others scurried around like beavers, gathering sticks to pile in front of the lodge. Running Crane did not understand why, but not wanting to admit his ignorance, he gathered sticks, too.

Reaching the top of the slope with the returning scouts, Wolf Eagle stepped to the pile, hauled back his leg, and gave a mighty kick. Sticks flew everywhere. A thick one bristling with sharp points flew straight at Running Crane's face. He caught the stick more by reflex than by intent, then gazed stupidly at the blood seeping from the punctures in his hand. Despite the pain, he could not let go. The others grabbed as many as they could.

As lazy as he acted around camp, Weasel Rider scrambled furiously and retrieved more sticks than anyone else. He could not hold them all, however, and several fell to the ground. When he stooped to pick them up, he lost several more. Finally he dropped the rest and stood over them, moccasins planted wide apart, arms crossed.

"Why did you stand still?" Beaver-Slaps-Tail-Twice asked Running Crane. "Do you not want to capture many horses?"

"This one will be enough," Running Crane answered. The words came forth unbidden, but they had a ring of truth.

Owl Child heard. His eyes swiveled first, then his head. Then he walked to stand directly in front of Running Crane and examined the hand holding the stick. Blood from the punctures seeped from between Running Crane's fingers, but he still clutched the stick tightly.

"You have strange medicine, Siksika," Owl Child declared.

Hunts-Smoke-Rising also came and looked. He

grunted with evident understanding, as did Otter, but they offered no words of explanation. Their interest both stunned and bewildered Running Crane.

"I shall take many horses," Weasel Rider proclaimed, brandishing sticks from his pile. "A horse for every stick."

Suddenly Running Crane understood. Each stick foretold a horse he might capture. In his ignorance, he had retrieved but one, and that one entirely by accident. He hid his chagrin behind a mask of satisfaction, but his heart sank. Once more his lack of medicine came to haunt him, and Owl Child's mysterious words slithered unnoticed from his mind.

"Tell us what you have found," Wolf Eagle commanded.

"Snake People camp half a day to the south," said Owl Child. "Between the rivers where they meet."

"How many tipis?"

"Twenty-three."

"They are a large band," Wolf Eagle said. "Do they have many horses?"

At this, Owl Child grinned broadly. "More than they deserve."

"They have one horse . . . ," Hunts-Smoke-Rising began, breaking his customary silence, but he did not continue.

Otter turned to Owl Child. "What kind of horse can make Hunts-Smoke-Rising speak when he has no need?"

"A stallion the color of the moon before snow comes," Owl Child said.

"That sounds like the spirit horse we have heard about," said Small Dog.

Running Crane's heart began to thump.

"This horse is very big and very wild," Owl Child continued. "You should hear him scream. Someone has whipped him many times. We could see the marks, but his spirit remains unbroken."

"Only fools whip a spirit horse," said Beaver-Slaps-Tail-Twice.

Owl Child went on, "We watched Snake warriors try to ride the stallion. Even with four men clinging to the ropes, none could stay on for three jumps. He tried to trample the ones he bucked off. Spirit horse or not, the stallion knows how to kill."

"They are stupid to try to ride him on hard ground," opined Otter. "They should lead him into the river before they try. Then if he throws them, they will land in the water. Besides, the water will tire the horse more quickly."

"The river bottom where they camp is rocky," said Small Dog. "A horse could break a leg."

"Dangerous rapids lie downstream from where the

rivers meet," Wolf Eagle said. "If the current carried a man that far, the river would mash him upon the rocks the way we mash berries for our pemmican. Where do they stake out this horse?"

"In the very heart of their camp, beside the largest tipi," answered Owl Child. "They use two halters instead of one, and two ropes. One rope leads inside the flap. They may not ride that horse, but they do not wish to lose him."

"What more?"

"They let no other stallion near because this one screams and wants to fight. That is good for us because they keep the buffalo-runners among the outer lodges. That way the spirit horse will not pass without a challenge. They drive the common horses to night pasture between the rivers."

Wolf Eagle thought for a time, then spoke. "We shall take the stallion, spirit horse or not," he said. "The stallion's medicine favors us by making the Snake People keep their buffalo-runners away. Those we shall take first. Then we shall take the spirit horse and make the Snake People cry. We shall take as many horses as we can. We will have to drive hard to get away, and we will surely lose some. When we reach the north, only then will we decide how to divide the herd."

The others spoke in agreement.

"Who will take the spirit horse?" Weasel Rider demanded.

"This stallion will kill gladly," said Otter. "We must use great care if we drive him."

Owl Child agreed. "The Snake People will follow like hungry wolves to recapture this one."

"Perhaps we should cut the horse loose and let him go where he will," offered Small Dog. "He might follow his mares when we drive the herd off, or he might lead the Snake People away from us."

His suggestion sparked another round of debate.

Weasel Rider hung on every word, eyes glittering. "Who will take the spirit horse?" he repeated rudely.

"A *warrior* will take the stallion," Wolf Eagle said, and Running Crane knew Wolf Eagle meant himself.

Weasel Rider's face darkened. He said no more, but Running Crane could see schemes whirling behind his scowl.

"We will approach their camp this night and watch tomorrow from hiding," Wolf Eagle said. "We will observe their every move." He looked upward, appraising the whitish feathers of cloud streaming from the west, and grinned. "Tomorrow night the clouds will swallow the starlight, and rain will favor us. We will pass unseen. The spirits smile upon us."

With that, he entered the lodge to get his war paint

and medicine. One by one, the others followed his lead.

Wolf Eagle selected a level spot and laid out his war knife. He painted himself before he appealed to the sun, most powerful among the spirits, to grant him help in taking horses and reaching home safely. Then he sang his wolf song.

The others also put on their war paint and sang their wolf songs, all save Running Crane, who retreated to the edge of the camp. He had no courage song to sing, and fear coursed through him more strongly than ever before, more strongly even than when he faced the tawny black-horn bull. He spoke to the sun, but he had little confidence his appeal would attract the sun's attention without the aid of strong medicine. He trembled and wished he could go home without forever branding himself a coward and a bearer of misfortune.

After Red Calf sang his own songs, he came to Running Crane. "Something troubles you," he said.

"I feel afraid," said Running Crane.

"I feel afraid, too," Red Calf told him. "So do the others. You do not walk alone with your fear."

"But I have no medicine," Running Crane explained.

Red Calf understood, and he left Running Crane to wrestle with his fears alone.

✳   ✳   ✳

Taking every precaution, Wolf Eagle used most of the night to approach the Snake encampment. His plan to arrive at the dark of the moon bore fruit, for thick clouds obscured the stars, and the night grew black as char.

The first gray of dawn found the party hiding in a secluded hollow Hunts-Smoke-Rising had found. Here the warriors left the boys while they climbed to a nearby height from which they could observe the Snake People.

Running Crane felt disappointed he could not go with the men. Even though he knew he could never capture such a creature, he wished to see this spirit horse who raced at such breathtaking speed through his imagination.

Weasel Rider opened his pack to consult his medicine. Only then did Running Crane remember that he had failed to retrieve his spare moccasins, oddments, and jerky from their hiding place. Had his lack of medicine begun working against him? He wished he knew. He consoled himself with the thought that he could ride one of the captured horses home. Then, perhaps, the moccasins he wore might last.

Weasel Rider sang his war song several times, then stole away in the direction the warriors had taken. A short time later he returned to the hollow, flushed with anger.

"They sent me back," he complained. Suddenly his face lit. "I have seen the spirit horse. Never have I seen such a creature. Strong medicine — a stallion too wonderful to be flesh alone."

Running Crane wanted to ask more about the spirit horse, but he clamped his jaws. Weasel Rider would only sneer.

Then Weasel Rider began to boast. "If Wolf Eagle fails to take the spirit horse, I will not fail," he proclaimed. "I will capture many horses," he added, as if repeating himself would make his boast come true. "You saw how many sticks I gathered. How many did Running Crane get? One, and the stick made him bleed."

"I saw how many you dropped, too," said Red Calf.

"That does not matter," Weasel Rider contended. "We will lose some horses the first days after a raid when we push hard to escape. Raiders always do. The more we drive off, the fewer the Snake People will have to pursue us."

Running Crane tried to shut their talk from his ears. Wolf Eagle would not allow an untested boy to enter an enemy encampment to try to capture horses, would he? Not when he wanted to take the spirit horse himself. But if Weasel Rider did capture many horses, his endless boasting would make life among the Kainaa unbearable.

CHAPTER NINE

Disaster

When twilight faded, the warriors returned from their spying and held council. They decided to wait until almost dawn, then slip into the Snake encampment.

"We will take the buffalo-runners from the outer tipis first," said Wolf Eagle. "Red Calf and Weasel Rider will hold any horses the warriors wish and help run off the herd."

Hearing this, Weasel Rider puffed out his chest importantly.

Wolf Eagle went on, "Running Crane shall hold the horses I take."

Stunned, Running Crane did not know whether to feel proud that Wolf Eagle had selected him or apprehensive. Everyone knew of Wolf Eagle's skill at entering enemy camps, but they also knew he took the most difficult horses. What if he brought the spirit horse?

"What of the spirit horse?" Weasel Rider asked, voicing the question in Running Crane's mind.

"We shall clear a path for the spirit horse between the buffalo-runners to prevent a challenge that would awaken the Snake People," Wolf Eagle said. "I shall decide the right moment to take that one."

"But . . . ," Weasel Rider had the temerity to begin.

"I shall take the spirit horse," Wolf Eagle said, his voice suddenly commanding. Then he went to consult his war medicine once again.

Beaver-Slaps-Tail-Twice motioned for Running Crane to follow and set off toward a stand of cottonwood trees. He stripped bark off a young one and rubbed sap over his hands. Running Crane chose another small tree. The instant his knife pierced the bark, a pungent, sour-sweet aroma sprang forth. Beaver-Slaps-Tail-Twice applied the sap to his arms and body. Running Crane did the same.

"The others will use white sage," the warrior explained. "I like this. During cold winters when forage becomes scarce, we feed our horses cottonwood bark. Snake People must do this same thing, I think. The smell helps quiet the horses so they will follow strangers."

They returned to find Otter and Small Dog dividing the elk meat they had dried at the war lodge. All ate heartily, knowing they might not eat again for a long time.

"Save some for the dogs," Beaver-Slaps-Tail-Twice counseled. "Throw one a piece, and he stops barking to eat. Move away until he becomes quiet."

Weasel Rider sneered. "Running Crane will never get close enough to the Snake People to even hear a dog."

Running Crane resolutely saved some meat.

The two rivers formed a slightly curving chevron such as migrating geese make in the autumn sky. The Snake encampment lay between them, well guarded on two sides by the rushing water, but the Kainaa had rain as an ally. Wetness released smells of fertile earth and growing things to cover their scent, and it muffled their footsteps and the swish of grass against their legs.

Wolf Eagle left Red Calf and Weasel Rider between the encampment and the herd of common horses so they could help drive the herd away when the party made their escape. Stationing Running Crane beside a dense screen of alder brush growing on the bank of the northernmost river, the warrior handed the youth his two rawhide ropes before he stole away into the darkness.

Water dripped from Running Crane, but not only because of the rain. Fording the river, he had almost stepped on a foraging muskrat. When the panic-stricken creature squeaked in terror and scrambled away, Running Crane had lost his footing and fallen. His sodden pack began to chafe his shoulder. He shrugged off the strap and laid the pack on the grass, then looped Wolf Eagle's ropes over his quiver.

Running Crane had felt alone many times since the black-horn bull killed his father, but never so alone as now. Thought of what might happen if the Snake People found him twisted his stomach. He wanted to run far away to safety, but he remained rooted to the spot. Wolf Eagle trusted him.

Twice Wolf Eagle returned leading a skittish buffalo-runner and wordlessly handed the tether to Running Crane before sneaking back to take another. The cottonwood sap seemed to work, for the horses settled down quickly and began to crop the grass.

The first hint of dawn had just touched the low-hanging clouds when a dog barked in the Snake camp.

Running Crane went cold and turned to run. He caught himself, but his sudden start alerted the horses. They stopped grazing and tossed their heads nervously. The barking came from the very center of the camp, not near the edge where the warriors would be cutting loose buffalo-runners. Had Wolf Eagle decided to take the spirit horse? The dog fell silent, and Running Crane tried to quiet his fears.

The dog barked again. This time another joined in, and another. A horse whinnied shrilly, more scream than whinny. Shouts and war whoops rent the air.

Hooves raced toward Running Crane, pounding the rain-softened earth.

He tried to mount one of the captured buffalo-runners, but the horse shied away, snorting. The other reared, hooves striking out. Running Crane dodged, and an arm's length of tether tore through his fingers.

An instant later, a spectral shape emerged from the darkness. Something huge and pale thundered past. The spirit horse! More horses raced close behind, all riderless. The buffalo-runners Wolf Eagle had left plunged and reared. Running Crane released one and struggled to reach the other so he could mount, but the horse backed frantically. The rain-slicked rope tore through his fingers, and the horse raced away.

Running Crane had barely the blink of an eye to ponder how he would explain the loss to Wolf Eagle before he heard more running horses and war whoops. Yelping dogs followed. He could not hide from the dogs, nor could he outrun mounted pursuers. The vengeful Snake warriors had almost reached him.

Desperate, he threw himself into the alders. Branches whipped his face and clutched at him. He struggled to force his way through. The Snake horsemen were closing fast. A root caught his leg. He jerked free and fell headlong into the river. The splash seemed impossibly loud, but the riders tore past without slowing.

The icy shock of snow-melt water drove all panic from Running Crane. He had to think to survive. He let the current carry him downstream until the horses passed, then pulled himself onto the bank. Water from his quiver splattered noisily onto the mud. A muskrat squeaked — his heart missed a beat.

He could not go upstream in the river. The current ran too strong and the rocks were too slippery. And the Snake People would concentrate their pursuit in that direction. He could not cross the river or drift downstream. Daylight was coming too fast. A woman getting water might discover him, or a dog, or a child. A boy with a rabbit-bow could skewer him easily in the water.

If he slipped safely past the camp to where the rivers met, open water lay beyond and someone would see his silhouette against the glowing dawn. Downstream, the rapids waited.

If he had felt alone before, now he felt like the only Siksika on the face of the earth.

A dog found his pack at the edge of the tangled alders and barked eagerly. Running Crane fumbled for the pouch of meat at his belt. The water-soaked rawhide refused to yield. He drew his knife, cut open the neck, and threw the meat in the direction of the dog. Too late. Other dogs raced to join the first, yelping furiously.

Running Crane slipped into the water again and floated downstream a few lengths, bringing the enemy camp that much closer. Generations of muskrats had tunneled into the bank here, and the river had undercut the edge. A margin of alder roots and thick prairie sod overhung the water, leaving the narrowest of air spaces between. Running Crane rolled onto his back so he could breathe, grasped a root, and pulled himself beneath the overhang.

Snake warriors arrived, shouting as they urged the dogs through the alders.

The current dragged at Running Crane's quiver, and the root he clutched started to pull free of the mud.

Farther and farther the root bent. His hand began to slip, but he could not roll over far enough to catch hold with the other, not if he wanted to keep his nose above the water. A dog yelped directly over his head.

The root gave way, and the current began to drive Running Crane downstream beneath the overhang. He probed the bank frantically, searching for another handhold. At any moment the air space might disappear. He might drift into the open.

The yelping dog followed above him, step by step.

His fingers found another root. He grabbed and clung with all his strength. The root sagged, held for a moment, gave way with a twang like a bowstring, then held again. The noise drove the hunting dogs into a frenzy, and warriors' shouts joined in.

Death has found me, Running Crane thought. Time slowed to a crawl. He felt strangely calm now death had come to him. But he held on.

The strained root twanged again, and a sudden chorus of muskrat squeaks erupted. The dogs redoubled their yelping as the root sliced through the river-softened mud and into a muskrat burrow. A panic-stricken muskrat bolted forth among the dogs. They tore the luckless creature to shreds and fought over its pitiful remains.

The warriors' fierce war whoops changed to shouts

of angry disgust. Their accursed dogs were hunting muskrats. Dogs kiyied as the warriors drove them away, and the hunt moved on.

Only when the danger had passed did Running Crane realize the water had chilled him so much he could barely move. His hand began to slip. This time he could not make his fingers obey. He held on as long as he could, but the root slid from his grasp and the current began to drive him along. Finding a rock with his foot, he managed to lever himself out into the glowing dawn.

The rain had stopped, and the sun burned bright behind the thinning clouds. After the dimness under the sod, the glare blinded him. He squinted hard. Not twenty lengths downstream, the undercut bank gave way to a wide area of gravel flat where the Snake People brought their horses to drink. Right beside him grew the last clump of alders before the opening.

Oblivious to the noise he made, he dragged himself ashore and plunged into the heart of the thicket, where he sank into a shivering heap. Before he could catch his breath, a group of boys brought horses to the river. Had they seen him? No. He curled into a ball and held perfectly still. He could only hope no Snake People would think to look for him this close to their lodges.

Snake boys led horses to drink many times, but the

sun took a long time to warm Running Crane sufficiently for him to notice that the horses they brought were not of the best. Owl Child had spoken glowingly of the size and quality of the Snake herd. Boys should drive common horses like these to the river to drink, not lead them. Had his party taken the best horses? Or did the Snakes ride their buffalo-runners in hot pursuit?

CHAPTER TEN

The Hungry Trail

The day lasted longer than any Running Crane had ever lived. The sun seemed to hang in the sky without moving. The river flowed three strides from his hiding place, but he dared not expose himself to drink. Hunger pinched his belly. Water had soaked his bowstring and made it useless. The feathers on his arrows had come adrift. His knife rusted before his eyes. His moccasins hardened into misshapen lumps. He had lost his sleeping roll. Ants crawled from the warming earth and nipped at him. Mosquitos tormented him.

He should have felt miserable, but he savored being alive. He felt neither excited nor fearful when the sun finally set. Night came. He had lived through this day. Tomorrow he would see the sun rise again. He could ask no more.

He pondered trying to work his way upstream along the bank in the darkness, but packs of dogs still roamed the area. Crossing the river here, he might fall and give himself away. Instead, he crept into the water and floated silently past the tipis and the cooking fires of the Snake People. The rumble of the rapids grew louder. As soon as the Snake encampment receded from view, he scrambled for the far shore.

Time and again he fell on the slippery rocks. The powerful current carried him into deep holes from which he emerged choking and sputtering. Each time he lost his footing, the river swept him farther downstream and the rapids roared louder. Each time he gritted his teeth and drove himself onward. He worked his way to shallow water, then to the bank. When he finally dragged himself ashore, chilled and shaking, the rapids roared almost at his feet.

Safe on solid ground, Running Crane tried to orient himself. The thin sliver of new moon, the moon-of-flowers, had hung briefly in the evening sky. Backbone-of-the-World hid it now, but the stars shone bright. When he located the Seven Brothers and the Star-That-Never-Moves, he knew north. Against the horizon, he could descry the shadowy foothills where he and his companions had built their war lodge.

He climbed the densely wooded slopes before daylight. Taking a circuitous route, he crossed over the ridge to stalk the war lodge from the back side as he would have stalked a wary deer. Reaching it, he waited and watched.

The lodge appeared unchanged. The ground they had worn bare going in and out showed no moccasin tracks made after the rain. He could see no sign that anyone had visited during his absence.

Once certain no enemies lay in ambush, he almost rushed into the lodge, but he resisted the urge. He had been careful to leave no tracks as he approached. He did not want to start leaving footprints now, even though he had not really rested for two nights and a day. Better to wait at a safe distance, hoping someone from his war party would return.

He backed away and hunted out the fallen tree where he had hidden his spare moccasins and his meager supply of dried meat. Weasel Rider's threats had helped him in the end. He thanked his fortune he had a spare bowstring, and the soft moccasins felt good on his feet after the chafing of the water-hardened ones. A drip of rain had found his jerky. Although the dried meat had begun to spoil, he ate immediately. The jerky tasted bitter, but only his tongue complained, not his empty stomach. Fed and exhausted, he crawled beneath the log and dozed.

A screaming jay woke him. Slipping to the edge of the ridge, he crouched in a patch of oak scrub. Voices came, low and indistinct. Snake People — or had the Kainaa warriors returned to look for him? He could not risk revealing himself until he made certain. Did the Kainaa know he would return to the camp? What if they went on without him? Should he wait until they left, then try to discover which way they went? Would he be able to follow if they covered their trail?

A voice called from nearby, and Running Crane's heart almost stopped. The voice spoke a tongue he did not know. A Snake scout was working his way along the ridge looking for sign — directly toward his hiding place.

Too late, Running Crane wished he had run when he had the chance. Now he knew how a jackrabbit felt hiding behind a tuft of prairie grass, wondering whether the hunter had seen him. Should he flee, or sit still?

Another voice called. The scout stopped and cupped his hand to his ear. Running Crane gathered himself to bolt. By racing directly down the hill, he might reach cover before the scout could send an arrow. Then he would have to run as fast as he could. He might escape, or he might not, but better to die running than to be caught sitting like the rabbits he had killed. *Five more steps*, he told himself.

The scout started toward him again. One. Running Crane let out the breath he had been holding and sucked in another. Two. The air felt thin and insubstantial. Three. It refused to fill his lungs. Four. Another call came from the direction of the war lodge. The scout stopped. He looked piercingly around, then turned back.

Running Crane could hardly believe his good fortune. For a second time, the enemy had almost found him then turned away. Still, he did not move. After a while, he heard the warning cries of a jay far down the hill in the direction of the creek where he had gathered willow wood.

He waited quietly until all sounds ceased. As much as he yearned to go back to the war lodge and search for anything useful, he did not. Instead, he gathered up what remained of his pack and moved one step at a time down off the ridge until he found a sheltered hollow. There he slept until the sun sank behind Backbone-of-the-World.

When he awoke, he thought about trying to find another enemy camp and horses he might capture. Perhaps if he knew more about horses, if he had more experience raiding, he decided. But not now, not alone.

He would miss the warriors and Red Calf, but if they yet lived, nothing he could do would find them. If the Snake People had caught them, he could do nothing except mourn. Weasel Rider he would neither miss nor mourn. But despite the persecutions, Running Crane found he could not wish Weasel Rider ill at the hands of the Snakes.

He worked his knife from its sheath, which had warped badly from repeated soakings, and pounded the leather with a rock until it softened. Then he polished the knife with fine sand and honed the edge on the bottom of a water-stiffened moccasin. Wolf Eagle's two ropes had also stiffened to uselessness. He thought of discarding the ropes, but he told himself Wolf Eagle would want them.

He straightened his arrows, then cleaned and sharpened their iron points. The fletchings had suffered greatly in the water, and he needed to replace them. Having no others, he rebound the feathers as best he could.

As if to listen to the rumbling of his empty stomach, an inquisitive ground squirrel ventured from a burrow and sat on its haunches.

Running Crane strung his bow without rising and waited with his eyes closed to slits as if he slept. *I shall kill you, little brother,* he thought, *only because I need your flesh to feed my own.* In one motion, he pushed his bow and loosed an arrow. Now he would have fresh meat and new strength beneath his belt when he walked. He ate everything but the skin and bones.

A stranger in this country, Running Crane knew his way only vaguely. He would have to travel at night, following the stars. He decided against trying to retrace the war party's earlier route. Enemies might be searching there. He would keep to the relative safety of the forest, close to the margin of the prairie, although that path led far to the westward of his destination. Even then he would not be safe. If Snake People did not find him, predators might, wolves or a cougar or grizzly. Once he had traveled well into Kainaa hunting grounds, he would travel by day. But he would still have to take every precaution to remain hidden.

He waited for the birds to settle on their roosts for the night before he set forth. The broken terrain at the base of the hills proved much more difficult to cross than the open prairie they had traveled on their way south. He had to climb steep banks and cross deep ravines with rushing streams at their bottoms. Whenever he forded, he thought of the river beside the Snake camp and shivered.

CHAPTER ELEVEN

Almost a Meal

A vulture circled low over the top of a nearby cliff, then landed. Below lay a narrow canyon, far too confined for the vulture's liking. Ungainly on the ground, the big bird hopped to the edge and peered downward, swaying its featherless head and croaking impatiently. A vulture meant something dead — or about to die.

Running Crane's empty stomach drove him from beneath the trees to investigate. Not wanting to expose himself against the skyline, he wormed his way on his belly. The vulture hissed at him, feathers rattling in threat. The gray-tipped black wings spread wider than

Running Crane stood tall, but he kept crawling. Finally the vulture flapped over the edge, croaking angrily.

Running Crane listened. Did enemy hunters wait? A gentle breeze ruffled the grass but brought no hint of voices. Slithering to the edge, he peered downward and almost whooped for joy. A buffalo had fallen over the opposite cliff to perish on the rocks below. It must have fallen recently, for no scavengers had yet torn at the carcass. Despite the possibility Snake People lurked nearby, Running Crane had grown too hungry to wait for nightfall.

The sheer rock walls dropped almost vertically. To reach the buffalo, he would have to find a break in the cliff. Working his way along the rim, he found a crack in the rocky wall which led downward. A stream gurgled among large boulders at the bottom, making the going difficult, and he had to leap from boulder to boulder to make progress.

He groaned when he discovered the carcass belonged to an aged bull long past its prime. The flesh would be tough and stringy, but hunger would make anything taste good. Working quickly, he peeled back the hide between the buffalo's forelegs and cut off a strip of meat. He chewed furiously, stopping only to drink from the stream. As he ate, he cut more strips which he laid aside. With the air in the canyon damp and the walls too steep for the sun's rays to reach the bottom, he would dry the meat after he climbed out.

Concentrating on food, he failed to keep a careful watch for danger. Then the wind blowing down the canyon brought the sound of a rock turning over. Belatedly cautious, Running Crane stood slowly to look around. Among the boulders, barely fifty paces away, he saw a grizzly.

Head swinging side to side, the bear sniffed, but the wind was blowing toward Running Crane; the huge creature could not smell him. He ducked low and began to back away. He could not outrun the bear, even dodging among the rocks, but this long-clawed one might stop to eat from the buffalo.

The bear huffed to clear her nostrils, then made a hollow, moaning call. An answer came from down the canyon. A cub. No, two half-grown cubs, downwind. Running Crane knew they would soon scent him — if they had not scented him already. The big one, a sow, had to be their mother. Perhaps the buffalo had fallen while trying to escape the bears. The sow had gone up the canyon looking for a path to the bottom, and the cubs had gone the other way.

Running Crane knew fear again. Nothing in the world of the Blackfoot posed greater danger than a sow grizzly with cubs. Nothing.

No trees in the canyon grew big enough to offer safety, and the bears were coming closer. Trapped, Running Crane realized his only escape lay up the canyon wall. Where? A narrow crack in the rock angled upward, his only chance. He leaped and jammed his hands into the opening. The sow heard him and grunted hoarsely to call her cubs. Fear gave him strength he had never known before. Pulling himself upward, he searched with his toes for a hold. He found one, then another.

Fierce growling from below drove him higher. A loose stone slipped beneath his hand. Flipping it away in a shower of shards and gravel, he looked down and saw the sow rise on her hind legs, straining to reach him. The stone struck her nose. She dropped back on all fours, shaking her head.

The crack narrowed to a seam. Running Crane scrabbled for another handhold, but the cliff face rose smooth above him. He could climb no higher. The sow rose on her hind legs again, swiping at him with claws longer than his fingers. He felt a tug on his legging and tucked his feet up tight beneath him. Stretching to reach him, she stood her tallest. Her claws grazed his moccasin. He had to get higher.

His toes found support, and he forced himself upward, trembling with the effort. He snared a handhold, then saw a projection off to the side. To reach it, he had to abandon his position and swing. If he missed, the waiting grizzlies would finish him quickly.

Fatigue ate at his muscles. He had to move or fall. He took a deep breath and swung. His toe caught the projection, slipped, then steadied. Moving his hands sideways bit by bit, he centered himself over the projection. He found another, higher toehold and pushed himself upward onto a tiny ledge invisible from below and barely wide enough to stand on.

He leaned against the cliff for a few moments, gasping for breath, then edged along the narrow shelf, his face and stomach pressed to the stone. The grizzly kept pace below, snuffling.

Unable to get at their quarry, the cubs began to wrestle. A gust of wind eddied down the canyon, rich with the scent of dead buffalo. They rose on their hind legs and sniffed, then started toward the meat. The sow gave a final throaty grunt and joined them.

Running Crane had to follow the ledge. After some distance, the cliff leaned back, and traveling became easier. Eventually the ledge crossed a trail that led down from the rim to the canyon floor. Faint claw marks in pebble-filled pockets showed the grizzly cubs had come that way.

Fed by hidden springs, the stream flowing in the canyon's bottom had grown. Running Crane pushed his way through the willows at its edge and drank deeply, then noticed a fiery pain in his leg. He was surprised to find three deep scratches running from just below his knee halfway to his ankle. In his excitement, he had not felt them. If those claws had gripped and held . . .

He dared not go back up the canyon to climb out where he had entered. The bears remained too close. If he climbed out here, the sow might find his scent trail and follow. Wading in the flowing water would hide his scent. He took off his moccasins and stepped into the stream.

When the canyon opened onto the prairie, Running Crane decided he had waded far enough. If his good fortune continued, the grizzlies would stay with the buffalo carcass. Still, they stood between him and the safety of the wooded hills. He wished he had some of Owl Child's bear medicine to keep them away.

The wind blew briskly from the mouth of the canyon, urging him out onto the undulating grasslands, away from the bears. The wind having served him well, he did not question it now. Before he started, he took time to strip bark from a willow and chew it, then rubbed it on his leg to lessen the burning and help the scratches heal. For the rest of the day, he kept the wind at his back and walked northeast, careful to leave no broken grass or bent stalks to mark his passing. At each rise in the land, he scouted carefully, never showing his silhouette against the sky.

When his shadow grew long and marched before

him in the dusk, he found a sheltered coulee. At the bottom of the steep-walled ravine ran a trickle of water. He drank and slept. Early the next morning he killed a prairie dog. While he ate, an old buffalo skull caught his eye. The sun had bleached the skull white, drying the horns and causing them to peel. Something about the skull seemed important, and he stared at it, trying to think. Then he remembered Wolf Eagle's ropes still tied to his quiver, hard and stiff.

He passed the end of one through the skull's eye sockets. Placing his foot between the horns to hold it down while he worked, he began to saw the rope back and forth. When he remembered Weasel Rider calling him an old woman, he laughed. If softening rope this way made him an old woman, so be it. After his many narrow escapes, nothing so foolish as Weasel Rider's name-calling would ever bother him again.

Working both ropes pliable took a long time, and Running Crane decided to spend another night in the same place. He hunted and slept with a full belly, but he dreamed troubled dreams of sitting rabbits and running horses and buffalo, and of walking for endless days and nights. Dream as he might, however, no sacred creature came to instruct him or offer medicine. He tried to make sense of the images when he awoke, but they grew confused and faded quickly.

CHAPTER TWELVE

Trail of the Spirit Horse

As Running Crane worked his way northeastward, the Backbone-of-the-World sank into the sea of waving grass behind him. Ahead, empty prairie stretched on forever. Each new roll in the land looked like the preceding one, and like the one that followed.

Running Crane paused to gather sarvice berries, but they had not ripened yet. Then he killed a grass bird. Not daring to risk a fire to cook it, he ate it raw as he walked. He would keep moving, searching for sign, watching the horizon constantly for smoke or a dust trail.

As twilight thickened, a horse appeared on the crest of a distant ridge, head held high, muzzle thrust strangely forward. A flank showed palest blue for an instant before the horse disappeared.

His mind spinning with excitement, Running Crane marked the spot. Although far away, the horse appeared large. And the color, like the moon-of-deep-snows . . . what if he had seen the spirit horse? Did the spirit work evil? Did Snake People follow it? Owl Child had said the stallion tried to kill any rider. Did the stallion also hunt men? And why did the horse hold his head high that way?

I could go closer, he told himself. *Even Hunts-Smoke-Rising spoke when he saw the spirit horse. If I have seen a horse the spirits watch over, I want to know that I have seen him.*

By the time he reached the spot he had marked, the light had failed, and he wondered whether he really had seen a horse at all. With the night too dark to search for tracks, he found a sheltered hollow. He chewed more willow bark and dressed the grizzly scratches again, then slept.

He rose at dawn and cast about for the horse's trail. When he found the hoofmarks, he marveled. They looked huge — a stallion then, and wandering alone. Still deep in enemy hunting grounds, he followed the tracks cautiously.

The sun had begun to sink by the time he peeked through the grass at the top of a ridge. Below lay a shallow depression that once held a small pond. The sun had drunk the last of its water, but the grass remained bright green. At its center grazed his quarry.

Running Crane held his breath as he gazed downward, fearing to make a sound. Never had he seen a more beautiful animal. Pale blue-gray with a dusting of black specks, the horse had a white mane. Its neck arched like a half-pushed bow, and its long tail brushed the grass. On its flank, he saw a strange, circular scar. Inside it, two bars lay crossed, the sign of the butterfly, bringer of dreams.

The stallion tossed his head oddly forward with every step. Did spirit horses always walk that way? When the horse raised his head to look for danger, Running Crane saw the two halters Owl Child had described. A length of rawhide rope trailed from each. Then Running Crane knew why the horse held his head strangely — to keep from stepping on the ropes.

He shivered with excitement. Not even in his dreams had the spirit horse looked so magnificent. And the pale blue-gray color . . .

He watched the stallion's every move until his heart ached with wishing for such an animal. Finally, when the light began to fade, he tore himself away. He hunted, killed, and ate, then settled in for the night.

Again a dream came to him. In this dream, the wind pushed him toward the stallion the same way it had pushed him toward the open plains. When he tried to leave the stallion and turn toward the hills, the grizzlies appeared to warn him away. When the stallion ran in a new direction, the wind shifted. No matter which path the stallion chose, the wind pushed Running Crane that way. When he walked toward the stallion, the wind slackened and seemed satisfied. If he ran, the wind blew hard in his face until he slowed to a walk again.

Waking, Running Crane knew he had dreamed a sacred dream. Even if the stallion did not prove a spirit horse, the wind of his dream had been a spirit wind. The spirit wind had taught him what to do. He would follow the stallion.

This time he did not have far to look. He found the stallion grazing beyond the first ridge. If any enemies lurked about, the stallion would have seen them. Even so, Running Crane kept low as he worked his way over the crest. The stallion's ears cocked toward him, but he continued to crop the grass.

Wolf Eagle's warnings about the stallion echoed through Running Crane's head, but the dream commanded. He stood slowly and let the stallion see him. The stallion shied away, his grazing interrupted. Whinnying shrilly, he loped toward the next ridge, head high. Running Crane followed, heart pounding with excitement. The stallion stopped once to look back, then crossed over the ridge. Eagerness overcame Running Crane, and he began to run. Then he remembered his dream and forced himself to walk.

When he reached the ridge, he saw the stallion grazing below. He slithered low over this crest, too, and stood. Again the stallion loped away. Again he followed, walking.

He followed all that day and most of the night, his way lit by the waxing moon. He walked. The stallion loped away, then stopped to graze. The stallion found a creek and drank. Running Crane slaked his thirst at the same creek. He slept before dawn, then found the stallion quickly. Still he followed, always walking.

The stallion could have run away and left Running Crane far behind, could have lost him easily. But, accustomed to the ways of men, he knew this lone man could not catch him. Any time he wished, he could turn and pound the man to a pulp with his hooves. Even so, men had strange, painful tricks. Best to leave them alone unless they attacked. And this man did not hurry, did not threaten.

The stallion wanted only to keep his distance. He meandered north, then west, then east a short way, then west, then north again. Day and night, Running Crane followed, keeping the stallion in sight, hunting and eating as he went. The stallion found grass and water, but never had time enough to graze or drink his fill. Running Crane followed too close.

The stallion grew hungry and thirsty. He grew thin, and his ribs began to show, but he also grew used to a human presence. He grazed longer when Running Crane appeared, letting the youth come closer before moving away.

Running Crane grew tired. His moccasins wore through, but he did not stop to patch them. He walked barefoot, one foot before the other. Time blurred. He neglected caution, forgot his fear of the Snake People. Nothing mattered but the stallion. He did not think about what he would do if the stallion let him get close. The wind of his dream had told him only to follow.

Four days after the moon began to wane, the stallion turned west. The summer sun burned hot, and lack of rain parched the land. Running Crane grew thirsty. A range of low hills lay ahead, and a sandy-bottomed watercourse crossed his path, its edges marked by deep-rooted cottonwood trees. Water would be flowing beneath the surface.

Running Crane thought about stopping to dig in the sand, but the stallion seemed to know where to go. He could smell water when Running Crane could not. They came to a steep-sided ravine where an ancient cottonwood tree had blown over, almost blocking the opening. A narrow game trail led past the leafless crown. The ravine made a sharp bend fifty paces beyond, and the stallion vanished from view.

Running Crane listened. Hooves on rock echoed forth briefly, stopping and starting without rhythm, tentative and confused. Then silence returned.

Suddenly hoofbeats pounded on the sand; the stallion was running directly toward Running Crane. Without thinking why he did so, he yanked at the thong holding Wolf Eagle's ropes to his quiver and jerked them free. The stallion thundered around the bend and ran straight for him. One rope in each hand, Running Crane waved wildly and shouted at the top of his lungs.

The stallion skidded to a halt barely ten paces away. His shrill whinny became a scream of frustration. Ropes! Ropes beat him when he bucked off riders. Ropes held him back when he wanted to fight other stallions. Ropes tried to trip him when he put his head down to eat or look where he was going. Ropes! The stallion spun around and raced back into the ravine.

The ravine has no way out, Running Crane realized. *I have him trapped.*

He tied Wolf Eagle's ropes across the opening, then gathered broken limbs and brush to fill the gap, working feverishly lest the stallion return. Confident the stallion could not break through at the trail, he piled more brush atop the long trunk of the fallen cottonwood.

Running Crane labored all afternoon in the hot sun until he had raised a formidable barrier. His mouth tasted dry and gritty. Wondering whether the stallion had found water, he climbed along the rim to look.

The ravine narrowed at the bend, then widened on the other side. Beyond, the sandy bottom ran another hundred and fifty paces before ending at a dry waterfall. The walls rose steep and smooth. A man could climb out, or a big-horned mountain sheep, but not a horse. Against the wall at the narrowest point of the bend nestled a spring, and beside the spring stood the stallion, glaring up at him.

Running Crane returned to the fallen cottonwood and sat in its shadow to ponder. He needed to drink, but the stallion guarded the spring. Leaves on the young cottonwood trees rustling in the wind reminded him: Cottonwoods need water. He began to dig. Half an arm's length down he found damp sand. He kept digging. When his fingertips could barely touch the bottom of the hole, he scooped out a trough to lie in as he worked. Water began to ooze into the bottom of the hole. He dug deeper and struck rock. A thin film of water seeped over it. He cleared more of the rock surface and found a small pocket which held barely a handful of water. Unless he wanted to spend as much time drinking as a horse spent grazing, he had to find more.

CHAPTER THIRTEEN

Standoff

Running Crane followed the ravine into the hills looking for water. Here and there, a cottonwood had taken
root, but the hills did not connect to the mountains.
Melt from the high snowfields that fed the prairie rivers
during the summer did not reach here. Water ran on the
surface only during rainy periods or in early spring
when the snows first melted in the low country. Half a
day's walk to the north, a line of dark green marked
where a small river snaked across the prairie — too far
away to go for a drink.

When he returned to the ravine, he found the

stallion cropping scattered clumps of grass. He had already devoured most of them.

"We make a fine pair, horse," said Running Crane. He looked thirstily toward the spring. Then he looked at the prairie. "You have all the water you can drink, but little grass to eat. I have all I can eat, but little water to drink. If you could talk, we could make a trade, I and you."

The idea of a trade grew stronger, and Running Crane gathered an armload of grass. He crawled under the trunk of the cottonwood, and peeked around the bend. The stallion stood at the far end of the ravine. Running Crane walked forward twenty paces, dropped the grass he had gathered, then retreated to the spring. He thought perhaps the stallion would eat long enough to allow him to drink.

The stallion shrilled and charged, ears laid back, teeth bared, hooves flashing, filling the ravine with his screams. Running Crane sprinted for the barrier. Sand sucked at his feet, and the dead cottonwood seemed to slide away from him. His breath came in ragged gasps. His thighs burned. Hoofbeats closed rapidly. He dove for the log and rolled under before the stallion could trample him.

The stallion shrilled in defiance and trotted off, satisfied with having driven the human away. When he reached the pile of grass, he stopped to eat. Running Crane tried again to trade his way to the spring with armloads of grass, with the same result. The stallion charged, intent on killing him.

Running Crane doubted the stallion understood the connection between the human he had chased and the grass. This spirit being was, after all, a horse. He gave up and returned to lie beside his seep. When the depression filled, he drank, but satisfying his thirst took a long time. In the morning, he hunted and ate, then returned to gaze at the stallion. The stallion glared back.

When Running Crane finally noticed Wolf Eagle's ropes under the brush he had piled over the game trail, he felt foolish for not remembering them sooner. He pulled one free and began to coil it. Seeing the rope, the stallion tossed its head and raced back to the spring, snorting. Running Crane pondered the stallion's reaction. And he remembered how the big horse stopped when he first blocked the trail. The stallion could have run him down easily. Then Running Crane realized the stallion did not fear him. The creature feared the ropes. But how much?

Running Crane crawled beneath the cottonwood and edged forward, ready to dive for cover. The stallion shrilled and charged. Running Crane waved the ropes over his head, and the stallion skidded to a halt, throwing up a shower of sand. Running Crane took another step, waving the ropes. The horse spun away and raced around the bend. His heart soaring in triumph, Running Crane hurried to the spring and drank his fill.

Now the youth knew he could drink and eat, but what about feeding the stallion? Leaving piles of grass would not tame a horse. He rubbed his lean belly thoughtfully. Food means much, he told himself, but water means more. He could stand by the spring and keep the stallion away, but he would need to sleep. Then he had an idea.

First, he gathered all of the brush, saplings, and dead branches he could find and threw them into the ravine. These he dragged to the narrow bend. The stallion charged again and again, but Running Crane waved the ropes to drive him back until he could build another barricade, this one between the stallion and the spring. Now if the stallion wanted to drink, he would have to drink from Running Crane's hand. If the stallion wanted to eat, Running Crane would have to feed him.

At first, the stallion refused to come near the barricade and stood at the far end of the ravine. Late in the afternoon, thirst drove the stallion to approach the barrier. Only then did Running Crane realize he had no way to give the horse water. Feeling foolish, he dumped the contents of his quiver on the ground and dipped it into the spring. Streams of water sprang through the stitching. The stallion sniffed suspiciously. He could smell the water and see it and hear it, but he snorted and galloped away.

Running Crane examined his leaking quiver. Even if the stallion had tried to drink, his muzzle would not fit within the opening. After a while, Running Crane thought of his shirt. He took his awl and sinew and patched the cuts that the spirit bull's hooves had made. Then he sewed up the armholes and the neck. He stretched the shirt over a forked branch and dipped it into the spring. The shirt dripped, but it would hold water long enough for the stallion to drink.

Thirsty, the stallion approached several times, but when Running Crane scooped up water, the horse snorted and fled. Remembering what Beaver-Slaps-Tail-Twice had told him, Running Crane peeled the bark off a young cottonwood and rubbed the sap over his hands and body. He daubed his shirt with cotton-wood sap, too. The smell helped calm the stallion. When the big horse approached again, still snorting distrustfully, he extended his muzzle and drank a few mouthfuls before shying away.

The taste of water intensified the stallion's thirst. He returned many times to drink, each time staying a moment longer. At last, he stayed long enough to drain the shirt completely, then moved only a few lengths away while Running Crane scooped up more. The next time, the horse remained beside the barrier and waited. Running Crane spoke in soothing tones and dipped water until the creature drank his fill. Then he offered a handful of dried grass. The stallion tried to bite his hand and grab the grass at the same time. Running Crane snatched his hand away, but he continued to talk softly. He offered the grass again.

The stallion seemed confused. This man did not act like the others. This man had rope, but did not whip him. This man did not run, did not shout. This man brought food and water. Gradually the stallion's mistrust diminished, and he accepted grass from Running Crane's hand.

For many days, the stallion had not eaten his fill because this human pursued him. Now he ate, and the supply of grass shrank rapidly. Soon Running Crane had to gather more. The stallion munched the grass as fast as he could bring it. Running Crane fed the stallion handful after handful until his arm ached from holding it out. He talked to the stallion until his throat grew raw.

He draped a rope around his neck and held the second rope in one hand while he fed the stallion with the other. He held a rope when he scooped up water for the stallion to drink. He laid the rope atop the barricade and held grass over it as the stallion ate. The stallion shied less often.

The trailing halter ropes dangled tantalizingly near. Frayed by the stallion's hooves, they would bear no strain, but Running Crane tried and tried to snare one. When at last he succeeded, he let the weakened leather trail across his open palm when the stallion pulled away. He repeated this process many times before he applied gentle pressure. When at last he held on, the stallion accepted the restraint.

All the while he kept feeding the stallion, Running Crane grew hungrier and hungrier. Eventually he left to gather berries and hunt. When he returned, he brought grass. The stallion whinnied in greeting and pranced expectantly at the barricade, waiting to be fed. The big horse had grown accustomed to his constant presence.

A sliver of the new moon-of-home-days hung low in the evening sky before Running Crane tried to tether the stallion. He prepared himself for a struggle, but the stallion accepted the restraint meekly. After that, events flowed quickly. Running Crane made a small opening in the barricade and went inside to feed the stallion. He patted the horse and led him around the floor of the ravine. He used a forked stick to curry the knots from the creature's mane and tail. When he returned from hunting or harvesting grass, the stallion greeted him with an eager whinny.

Next Running Crane tied the frayed halter ropes over the stallion's neck. He knotted one of Wolf Eagle's ropes to the halter and led the horse to water, then to graze. Had the stallion bolted, he could not have stopped him from escaping, but the stallion cropped the grass contentedly.

Running Crane stood alongside while the stallion grazed, rubbing and talking. He leaned against the stallion's side, glorying in the stallion's strength, his heart filling. No longer did aching loneliness haunt him as it had since his father walked the Wolf Trail.

When the time came, Running Crane feared what he must do. He feared the stallion would hate him. He feared he would be left alone once more. Still, he knew. The time had come for him to ride.

CHAPTER FOURTEEN

A Contest of Wills

Until he remembered that Owl Child said the stallion tried to trample fallen riders, Running Crane did not consider the danger in what he contemplated doing. The stallion acted tame enough, but how would he react to weight on his back? For a horse, the ability to buck off a mountain lion or pummel a wolf with slashing hooves meant survival. A horse's teeth and hooves could do terrible things to a man. Running Crane sought another dream to instruct him, but none came. The only sign came from the wind. The wind pushed him toward the stallion.

He delayed for another day. He could lead the stallion home, he thought. But the Kainaa boys would laugh because he had feared to mount. Or he could turn the stallion loose and abandon his dreams. Who would know?

He would know. The wind would know.

Once he reached his decision, Running Crane worked quickly. He fetched grass and blocked the path out of the ravine. While the stallion ate, he tied both of Wolf Eagle's ropes around his neck and tethered him. The stallion's ears flicked curiously, but he seemed unconcerned.

"I mean you no harm," Running Crane told the stallion. "I do not have loads to place on your back, heavier and heavier each day, until you are ready to bear my weight. That is what I would do if I led you to the encampment. I mean you no harm." With that, he swung himself lightly upon the stallion's back.

The stallion threw the boy with a single buck.

Running Crane landed with a resounding thud that knocked the wind out of him. He tried to roll clear, but he could not move. The stallion would trample him in an instant. He braced himself, ready for the end, but the end did not come. The stallion had thrown him beyond reach of the tethers. He spat the sand from his mouth and opened his eyes.

The stallion looked at him, ears cocked forward as if to ask, *What are you doing down there?* Then he resumed eating as if nothing had happened.

Running Crane regained his breath and staggered to the spring to rinse his mouth. When he returned, the stallion gave no sign of nervousness. Again he swung himself astride. Again the stallion threw him with a single effortless buck. Again he landed hard. Again the stallion resumed eating, unconcerned.

Twice more the stallion threw Running Crane before he gave up. Stiff and sore, he realized he was acting as hard-eared as the Snake People. If he wanted to mount the stallion, he should do it in water.

The next morning, aching with every step, Running Crane led the stallion north. When they reached the river, the stallion drank long and deep, then wanted to graze. Running Crane found a lush growth of grass but no trees close enough to tie the ropes. Not trusting a stake, he used his knife to cut a circle half the length of his forearm from the thick sod. Beneath the circle, he dug out a hole as deep as he could reach. He tied a rope around the hunk of sod, then drove the sod to the bottom of the hole. The stallion might break the rope, but he could never drag the sod up out of the hole by straining outward from the end. A human needed only to grip the rope short above the hole and then pull straight up.

To Running Crane's great disappointment, the river proved too shallow either to tire the stallion or to provide much cushion if — when — the stallion threw him, but he did find a pool with trees growing close to the water on both sides.

Water in the pool flowed not nearly as deep as Running Crane would have liked. A horse puts his head between his forelegs to launch a good buck. In shallow water, the horse would not have to plunge his nose deep beneath the surface to accomplish that. Still, the pool would offer a softer landing than dry sand.

When he returned with the stallion, he tied one of the ropes to a branch, then led the horse into the water. Crossing, he tied the other rope on the opposite side. He retied the ropes several times until he maneuvered the stallion to the center of the lazy current.

He had more difficulty mounting the stallion in the water because he had to jump and lie on his stomach across the horse's back before he could swing his leg up and sit astride. The stallion did not wait for that. He bucked immediately and sent Running Crane flying to land with a mighty splash.

On the third try, Running Crane managed to swing

himself astride. That time he held on during four bucks before he sailed high over the stallion's head and landed upstream. Thrashing frantically, he fought to regain his feet before the current carried him into reach of the stallion's hooves. One slashing hoof could pulp his skull like an overripe berry. Closer and closer to the stallion he drifted. Almost under the stallion's nose, he found the bottom. When he stood, the stallion neighed and reared. Running Crane clamped his eyes shut — and felt a soft nose pressing his chest. He opened his eyes to find the stallion gazing at him in wonderment.

What are you doing, you silly Siksika? the stallion seemed to ask. *Are we going to play the bucking game any more?* Tossing his head, he invited another try. This time he waited until Running Crane gained a firm seat before bucking him off.

Running Crane tried and tried. Sometimes he stayed on for a few jumps. Other times the stallion threw him immediately. But he climbed back on the stallion for one more try, then another, and another. The result did not change. Finally he gave up and led the stallion from the water. The horse would not let him ride.

Running Crane resigned himself to leading the stallion. If he could not ride, perhaps no one else could. He worked his way north and eastward in search of a track or landmark he might recognize. Each time he crossed a ridge, he grew more apprehensive, fearing an enemy would see him. He could hide himself, but not the horse.

The sea of grass turned golden under the summer sun. All the bands of the Kainaa would be gathering in the going-home-days encampment which the tribe always held before the great hunt. He wondered whether he could find them. More likely, wide-ranging scouts would find him first.

Late one afternoon, he led the stallion over a high ridge and began the descent toward an unusually wide bottom. Halfway down, he saw mounted warriors on the crest of a ridge to the west, black silhouettes against the setting sun. The warriors milled about, pointing and shouting. Looking into the blazing sunset almost blinded Running Crane, but he waved. Now he would not have to walk the rest of the way home. A moment later, the warriors whipped their horses and streamed toward him at a dead run.

The stallion laid back his ears and shrilled a challenge, then began to rear and jump. Running Crane had all he could do to hold on. The warriors had crossed the bottom and begun to climb the long slope before he had a chance to look closely at them.

He almost looked too late.

Snake People! That they rode horses here meant they were returning home after a raid. The Snakes recognized the stallion captured from their camp. Now they would reclaim him.

Running Crane had only one chance. He vaulted onto the stallion's back and dug his heels into the creature's ribs. The stallion reared, and Running Crane clung with all his strength.

Spine-chilling war whoops rent the air as the Snakes rushed in for the kill. The moment this foolish Blackfoot hit the ground, they would finish him. Then they would recapture their stallion.

The war whoops startled the stallion. He stopped rearing. Worse things than a rider threatened. When Running Crane mounted before, he had always tied the stallion; he never gave him the chance to run. Now the stallion ran, charging straight for the Snakes. They scattered like leaves before a whirlwind as he raced through them, shrilling challenges. War whoops turned to shouts of anger as the stallion left the Snakes behind, surging effortlessly over the ground until the pounding hoofbeats merged into an endless roll of thunder.

Running Crane bent low over the great horse's neck. The windblown mane whipped his face. Tears came to his eyes. His thighs ached from gripping, but his heart swelled. Never had he dreamed a horse could run so fast, not even this one.

He let the stallion run over the ridge and across the next bottom before trying to rein in. The stallion slowed to an easy lope, then to a walk. When Running Crane looked back, the Snake warriors had disappeared in the distance.

Running Crane patted the mighty stallion's neck and turned him northeast, toward home. He still did not know exactly how to get where he wanted to go, but he would no longer walk. He would ride, as befitted a Blackfoot.

CHAPTER FIFTEEN

Wolf Eagle

Once the stallion decided to end the bucking game, he allowed Running Crane to mount at will. The youth grew sore from the unaccustomed riding, but knowing the soreness would soon fade, he accepted it gladly. When he needed to hunt, he ground-tethered the stallion. The bowstring's twang made the big horse jump nervously the first few times he loosed an arrow close by. After that, the sound caused no reaction, not even when Running Crane sent arrows from the stallion's back.

Herds of buffalo roamed the prairie. Running Crane had tired of eating small game, but he could rely upon his bow for hunting nothing larger. The calves had already grown too big for a clean kill, and he would not send arrow after arrow into one hoping for a fatal hit. Still, he could not resist running buffalo with the stallion when he had the chance. Unafraid, the stallion would close with the largest bulls, responding to pressure from his rider's knees and leaving Running Crane's hands free to use his bow.

When Running Crane saw a flock of buzzards circling, he remembered the buffalo he had found in the canyon. Instead of landing on the ground, the buzzards stayed aloft or perched high in the tall cottonwoods that marked the course of a stream. Large to draw this many scavengers, whatever they were watching might still live. Or did a grizzly or a pack of wolves guard a kill and keep the buzzards at bay? Or had human predators brought it down?

Running Crane approached cautiously. Nothing could catch him in the open. The stallion ran too fast. But an arrow let fly from ambush could fell him before he knew an enemy hid close by.

After the glare of the sun-washed prairie, cool shade waited beneath the trees, dim and noisy with cicadas buzzing in the summer heat. Their noise forced him to depend upon the stallion's senses. He watched the flickering ears for any sign of danger. When low-hanging limbs forced him to dismount, he strung his bow, then nocked an arrow and led the stallion. A trio of long-tailed magpies scolded at him. Buzzards perching high in the top of a large cottonwood squawked, then flapped away. In the shadows at its base, whatever they had been watching lay in a heap.

The stallion showed no alarm, but he balked at going closer. Satisfied no imminent danger lurked nearby, Running Crane tethered the horse to a limb, then ventured toward the heap. The heap moved suddenly and groaned. A man. The man struggled to a sitting position and leaned against the tree trunk.

His bow half pushed, Running Crane edged nearer until he could make out the man's features. Suddenly he swallowed hard. After traveling so far, first alone, then with the stallion, he could hardly believe his eyes.

"Wolf Eagle?"

Wolf Eagle had remained aloof, keeping his own counsel. He had made no mention of Weasel Rider's bullying. He had seemed unaware of Running Crane's efforts around their camps. But the warrior *had* chosen him to hold captured horses. Running Crane shivered when he remembered losing them. What would Wolf Eagle think now?

Wolf Eagle croaked weakly, as if the mere act of speaking required too much effort. His eyes looked glazed, and a heavily scabbed cut ran from a lump on his left temple back past his ear. "I see Running Crane, or I see his ghost," he whispered.

"You see Running Crane."

Wolf Eagle grunted, his lips dry and cracked. "Thirsty," he murmured.

Running Crane hurried to the creek.

After Wolf Eagle drank, he closed his eyes and leaned back. No limbs seemed broken. The cut on his head appeared to be healing. His pack, his bow, and his quiver lay beside the tree. He wore a belt, but the sheath for his war knife hung empty. Dark patterns of dried blood mottled his hands, and scuffed tracks showed where he had crawled more than once toward another tree and back. If injured, why did he crawl in that direction instead of to water?

Moving carefully, Running Crane went to look. He found a bloated mare emitting the stench of the long dead. One broken foreleg jutted at a strange angle. Her throat gaped open. Wolf Eagle had ended her suffering cleanly. His war knife lay half hidden beneath a haunch.

Running Crane picked up the knife and scrubbed away the blood with dry sand, then returned to Wolf Eagle. The injured warrior needed food and more water first. Later he might choose to tell his story.

Running Crane ground-tied the stallion in a patch of tall grass, then hurried off to hunt. When he returned with two white-tailed jackrabbits, he found Wolf Eagle's flint and steel and started a small fire, despite the risk enemies might scent the smoke.

Smelling the roasting meat, Wolf Eagle opened his eyes and groaned hungrily. Running Crane fed him small pieces until he would accept no more. He finished the rest himself, eating his first cooked meat in a long time and enjoying the fire.

Wolf Eagle slept most of that day and the next, awakening now and again to eat and drink. When Running Crane tried to help him lie down, he groaned and insisted on propping himself against the tree.

"Cannot lie down," he mumbled. "Cannot stand up. Everything moves."

Running Crane made him as comfortable as possible with a backrest of limber branches padded with grass, then went to tend the stallion and hunt.

This time Wolf Eagle fed himself.

Buzzards flapped down from the trees to tear at the dead mare, and the stench grew steadily worse. Running Crane did not want to remain near the carcass, but Wolf Eagle obviously could neither walk nor ride. The Blackfoot did not consider cottonwoods the best of trees for making a travois, but no lodgepole pines grew nearby.

He used Wolf Eagle's knife to cut two saplings long enough and serviceably straight. The dead mare's bridle and one of Wolf Eagle's ropes served to lash the travois together. He wove a platform of branches, then fashioned a tall backrest for Wolf Eagle to lean against. Wolf Eagle's robe and chest strap made harness for the stallion. A ride along the bottom and back dragging the travois assured Running Crane the stallion would not bolt.

When he returned, Running Crane found Wolf Eagle sitting erect. The warrior's eyes had cleared.

"You feel better," Running Crane said.

"I feel better," Wolf Eagle agreed. "I hurt my head. I do not know how. I remember riding many days. I saw Snake People, but they did not see me. I tried to ride down the bank. The mare broke a leg. I fell and hurt my head again. After that, I could not walk. I could not lie down. I could only sit."

"You cut the mare's throat."

"That I remember."

"I found this," Running Crane said. He handed the war knife to Wolf Eagle.

Wolf Eagle tried to put the big knife back in its sheath, but his hands shook. Running Crane steadied him.

"Where do we camp?" Wolf Eagle asked.

"I do not know," Running Crane told him. "My path

from the Snake People's camp has not been as the eagle might fly."

"Nor mine," said Wolf Eagle. A breath of wind brought the reek of the dead horse, and he wrinkled his nose. "My mare?" he asked.

Running Crane nodded.

Wolf Eagle struggled to his feet, but he paled and sank down again. "I have stayed here too long."

"I have a travois to carry you," Running Crane said. "Will you ride?"

Wolf Eagle assented, and Running Crane went to rig the travois. When he led the stallion back to where Wolf Eagle sat, the warrior's eyes grew round with wonder.

"The spirit horse," he exclaimed in awe. "Then you have walked the Wolf Trail, and I have died, too. Do we camp in the Sand Hills?"

"You remain among the living," said Running Crane. "The stallion breathes. A ghost does not ride him."

Understanding, Wolf Eagle cleared his throat. "You have a story to tell."

Running Crane agreed. "I have a story."

"I want to hear your story in a place which does not stink."

When Running Crane helped Wolf Eagle pull

himself onto the travois, the injured warrior swayed dangerously.

"Tie me," he ordered, resuming something of his habitual air of command now that he had made a decision.

Running Crane used the second of Wolf Eagle's ropes to lash him to the travois. Then he lashed Wolf Eagle's belongings to the back rest. The sun had already risen high when they started, but they stopped early so Wolf Eagle would not have to endure a long first day of travel. Sarvice berry bushes and a prairie dog town provided their evening meal.

After eating, Wolf Eagle seemed remarkably improved. "I know where we camp," he said. "I see Backbone-of-the-World on the horizon. I know the shape of these hills."

"You also know where the Kainaa will gather for the going-home-days encampment, then," Running Crane decided.

"We should arrive in five days," Wolf Eagle said confidently. "The time has come. Tell me your story."

"You brought me two fine buffalo-runners to hold," began Running Crane. "I let those horses get away."

"What happened, happened," Wolf Eagle replied, unperturbed.

Running Crane did not speak of his fears, but he omitted nothing else. When he spoke of the grizzlies, Wolf Eagle interrupted.

"So that is what happened to your leg?"

Running Crane raised the tattered flap of his legging. Three parallel scars showed white upon his calf.

Wolf Eagle hummed thoughtfully. He remained impassive as Running Crane spoke of his efforts to catch the stallion, then grunted when he heard of the youth's escape from the Snake war party on the stallion's back. "They were the same Snake People I saw," he concluded. "They had our horses, but only poor ones. We shall hear more of that when we return."

"Nothing else happened until I found you," Running Crane concluded.

"You did not fear the stallion?"

"I feared him," Running Crane said quietly.

"Yet you tamed him," Wolf Eagle observed. "You conquered your fear."

"Perhaps I did not conquer my fear," Running Crane said slowly. "The fear changed. I came to accept fear as part of me. Knowing he *could* kill me proved easier than fearing he *might* kill me."

"And you imagine you have no medicine." Wolf Eagle laced his words with skepticism, but he continued without waiting for an answer. "That is something I shall consider."

Running Crane waited for the warrior to say more, but a silence grew between them.

After some time, Wolf Eagle shifted to a more comfortable position and began to tell his own tale. He could recall nothing about what happened during the raid or how he received the wound on his head. He awoke to find himself riding the mare. He rode south from the Snake camp, then far out onto the prairie to evade pursuit. The route he had taken led him well to the east of their trail south. He remembered seeing the Snake warriors and the mare falling. He remembered cutting the mare's throat, and he remembered his head spinning when he moved.

"Do you know how the Snakes discovered our party?" asked Running Crane.

"No," said Wolf Eagle. "My memory of the raid is like an image reflected on running water. Little pieces flash here and there, but I cannot put them together to make a picture I can recognize. Nor can I see what lies beneath and disturbs the surface. I know only that something went very wrong. Others may have escaped. They will know things I cannot remember."

CHAPTER SIXTEEN

The Medicine Bull

Another day's travel brought no marked change in the land, but Wolf Eagle felt satisfied with their progress. After eating the marmot Running Crane killed and cooked, he felt well enough to grumble. "Ground-walkers are not fit food for a Blackfoot," he complained. "Snake People eat small creatures that run around on the ground. A Blackfoot should eat real meat — buffalo."

Running Crane agreed. "I have chewed on too many ground-walkers since we left."

Wolf Eagle slapped his belly. "I do not wish to

return with nothing but such creatures beneath my belt," he declared. "They may fill an empty stomach, but eating ground-walkers weakens a man. I need real meat to become strong."

"You see my bow," said Running Crane. "I could not kill a buffalo with that bow."

"I have wondered why you brought a child's bow," said Wolf Eagle, letting the question hang between them unasked.

"I could not find the bow Three Belts gave me," Running Crane answered.

Wolf Eagle grunted.

Next morning, the sun rose to reveal forerunners of a buffalo herd approaching their camp. More and more followed until shaggy black horns dotted the grass. A huge, tawny bull loomed conspicuous among them.

Wolf Eagle stared hard at the tawny bull, then turned to Running Crane. "I will wager my finest buffalo-runner against your old bow that those hooves fit the marks upon your shirt."

"I shall not make a trial of that," Running Crane responded uneasily. He did not need Wolf Eagle to remind him of the huge creature's efforts to kill him, or of his panic.

"I hunger for buffalo meat," said Wolf Eagle. "Kill one. Use my bow."

Running Crane warmed with pride that the great warrior would offer his bow.

Wolf Eagle examined the sinew bowstring to make certain it had not frayed. Satisfied, he tried to string the bow. He groaned mightily, and beads of sweat rose upon his brow. But he could not manage from a sitting position. He knelt shakily and tried again, groaning louder, then suddenly dropped the bow and held his head with both hands, moaning.

"If I try again, my head will fall off," he said. "You shall string the bow."

Running Crane hesitated.

Wolf Eagle thrust the bow at him. "String the bow!" he commanded.

Running Crane wrapped his leg around the bow, grasped the string, and heaved. The string crept upward toward the nock, stopped, then began to slip back down the bow.

"String the bow!" Wolf Eagle hissed.

Running Crane summoned every ounce of strength, and the string crawled slowly upward. Shaking with the strain, he forced the string into the nock. He eased the pressure slowly, making certain the string had seated properly, then gasped for breath.

"You do not know what you can do until you try," Wolf Eagle said, as if he had felt certain all along that

Running Crane would succeed. Handing him the quiver, he pointed to a small group of cows and calves grazing near the creek. "Kill a fat calf that we may eat like men."

Running Crane gazed at the herd, but he could not move. The fears he had felt when the bull chased him before came swarming back to paralyze his limbs.

"You wait for the buffalo to come closer," Wolf Eagle exclaimed contemptuously.

"A buffalo killed my father when he hunted on foot," said Running Crane finally. He tested the powerful bow and found he could draw an arrow only part of the way. Could he handle such a bow from the back of a running horse? "I shall ride."

"Buffalo have killed many who hunted on foot," Wolf Eagle said. "Buffalo have killed many who rode untested buffalo-runners on first hunts, too."

"I have tried the stallion against a running herd," said Running Crane. "He obeys me and has no fear."

Wolf Eagle gazed into the distance. "Hunting on foot would make your success more certain."

"What of the bull?" Running Crane asked.

"Your medicine has proven stronger than the bull's," Wolf Eagle said.

"I have no medicine," Running Crane protested.

Wolf Eagle flashed him an inscrutable glance. "Go,"

he ordered, once more the leader of a war party, even if it numbered only two. "Run the buffalo on the stallion if you will. I need real meat."

Wolf Eagle would accept no arguments. Running Crane either had to go or appear as one who seeks safety in the face of danger. He knew the taste of fear, but that did not make him a coward.

"I will ride," he said.

Sensing something about to happen, the stallion pranced nervously, flicking his ears back and forth. Once he saw the buffalo, he knew. Running Crane dug his heels into the stallion's ribs, and the great horse leaped forward.

The buffalo turned and ran. They gathered speed slowly, like an avalanche sliding down the side of a hill. The cows quickly forged ahead. The heavier bulls lumbered after them. Bawling calves brought up the rear, but they had grown big and strong during the summer. They overtook the slower bulls and ran among them, seeking protection. A choking cloud of dust boiled in their wake.

The stallion caught the herd easily. Despite the presence of bulls, he responded instantly to the pressure of Running Crane's knees. Moments later, horse and rider raced alongside a fat calf. Even at half draw, Wolf Eagle's bow had power enough to drive an arrow deep into the vital spot behind the calf's foreleg. The first arrow found the heart, and the calf tumbled end over end, giving a last despairing bawl.

Running Crane pulled away and waited for the rest of the herd to pass, then dismounted to butcher his kill. No sooner had he begun than the stallion began to prance and snort. Danger! Running Crane vaulted onto the horse's back just as a huge shadow emerged from the windblown dust — the medicine bull. The instant the bull saw Running Crane, the creature lowered his enormous head and charged.

The stallion sprang to the side, almost unseating Running Crane. The bull wheeled to follow, but slowed to a halt, then trotted back to guard the calf as if the death had resulted from his failure to protect the herd. Running Crane guided the stallion toward the bull, trying to draw it away. The bull charged only a short distance, then returned to the dead calf.

Running Crane knew he could catch the herd and kill another calf, but a spirit of battle moved in his heart. This medicine bull had almost killed him. As he circled the stallion, the bull whirled to face him. The great horse took up the battle with a will and seemed to taunt the lumbering creature by approaching nearer and nearer. The bull charged again, and the stallion dodged away.

Running Crane urged the stallion to an easy lope around the bull. The bull turned to follow, but became confused. He stopped, and Running Crane saw his chance. He veered the stallion toward the bull and raced past. Drawing Wolf Eagle's bow with a strength he never knew he had, he sent an arrow deep into the bull's side. The bull bellowed, but did not go down. The arrow had flown high. The bull whirled to charge, and Running Crane planted an arrow in the heart. The bull's forelegs buckled first. Then the huge creature fell slowly onto its side, bawling and kicking until death ended the struggles.

Wolf Eagle examined the scene with a hunter's eye. He noted that Running Crane had killed the calf with a single arrow, and he noted the two arrows deep in the bull's side.

"I respect your aim, Siksika," he rumbled.

"The stallion put me in position," Running Crane said. He stared at the fallen bull. Now the heat of the hunt had passed, a sadness came over him. "I wish now I had not killed the bull, but he would have killed me. He died well."

"Your medicine proved stronger," Wolf Eagle declared. "Perhaps the bull was meant as a test for you. He tested you before, and you lived."

Running Crane doubted, but he had no answer. He

butchered the calf. When they had eaten all they wanted, he cut strips of meat for drying.

"You killed a medicine bull, one of powerful spirit," said Wolf Eagle. "Take the hide and scalp. Let them become part of your medicine."

"I killed the bull," Running Crane said, "but the spirit horse's medicine, not mine, proved stronger."

Wolf Eagle humphed and looked exasperated. "A man should accept what honor the spirits offer him," he declared. "He should feel proud of his deeds."

Running Crane discovered he did feel proud, and he cut the wooly scalp from between the horns. Skinning the huge bull alone required great effort, but he used the stallion and Wolf Eagle's rope to roll it over. He removed the flesh as best he could and tied the hide to the travois. But the travois could not carry all the meat unless Wolf Eagle walked.

"I shall offer the meat of the medicine bull to the sun in thanks for his protection," Running Crane said.

Wolf Eagle grunted, approving. "I shall offer my thanks, too, for I have eaten well. My wives will scrape and tan the hide. If I must ride on a travois like an old person, at least the buffalo-runner who carried you to kill the medicine bull shall drag it."

CHAPTER SEVENTEEN

An Old Adversary

Before dusk, Wolf Eagle and Running Crane stopped in a small cottonwood grove to let the stallion graze. The day continued still and hot, and cicadas, countless flattened black shapes clinging to the trees, buzzed their never-ending refrain. Running Crane pondered how these small creatures could make so much noise.

"From here to the next good campsite is a day's travel," Wolf Eagle announced, nearly shouting to make himself heard. "One day and a half of a second beyond will bring us to the meadow where the Kainaa camp. I grow stronger each day. We shall arrive fit."

He tried to demonstrate his improvement by walking, but after a few steps he stumbled. The sudden movement made him dizzy, and he sat down abruptly. "My head spins when I move quickly," he muttered.

"Your head will mend," Running Crane assured him.

The stallion snorted. Standing at the end of his tether, he gazed toward a ragged growth of brush on the ridge overlooking the bottomland. Ears pricked forward, he shifted nervously. From where they sat, Running Crane and Wolf Eagle could not see what the stallion saw. Nor could anyone see them.

Wolf Eagle pointed silently at Running Crane, then at his own bow and quiver. Running Crane strung his old bow first and handed it to Wolf Eagle. Stringing the warrior's bow required all his strength, but he managed more easily than the first time. He nocked an arrow and drew three more from the quiver to carry points up in his bow hand. Wolf Eagle gestured toward the ridge.

Now Running Crane felt glad he had grown up on the margin of the northern woodlands where he had long practiced moving quietly through thick undergrowth. He slipped through the brush along the creek, then circled the ridge. Heart pounding, he had to take care not to let his breath hiss between his lips. He thought about going back and mounting the stallion, but he decided Wolf Eagle knew best.

Because the ridge curved sharply away from the campsite, Running Crane could remain in cover. No wind blew, but a leaf trembled in the center of the brush patch. Something hid there. Running Crane examined the slope beyond the ridge to make certain he did not turn his back on other dangers. A herd of grazing pronghorns showed no sign of alarm. Whatever the danger, it lay only in that brush.

A breath of wind whispered through the brush, covering the tiny sounds he made. Even so, he moved with infinite caution, crouching, placing one foot at a time, feeling carefully for sticks that might snap. A bush twitched close ahead as the intruder carelessly changed position.

Running Crane straightened ever so carefully and stepped forward, ready to loose an arrow. The figure he saw lying among the scrub looked ill-fed and unkempt, leggings tattered, hair a matted tangle of knots and dead grass. The figure rose slightly to peer toward the stallion. Remembering that Wolf Eagle became dizzy the moment he exerted himself, Running Crane could take no chances. He tensed to send the arrow, but something about the figure stayed him. Bow half pushed, he coughed.

The figure dropped flat and whimpered, arms outstretched.

Running Crane stood clear, ready for any sudden move. "Roll over," he ordered. If the intruder did not comply, that meant he did not understand the Blackfoot tongue — an enemy he would kill. "I want to see your face."

The figure squeaked and rolled face up, hands outstretched, whining for mercy.

Running Crane lowered the bow. "Weasel Rider!" he exclaimed.

Weasel Rider's whine changed when he recognized Running Crane. "Quiet," he hissed. He crouched and pointed. "I have found the spirit horse of the Snake People. I am waiting until dark to capture that horse. I will let you help me."

Running Crane slid the extra arrows back into the quiver. "I ride the stallion," he said. "Wolf Eagle watches him for me."

Weasel Rider squeaked like a muskrat. "Wolf Eagle?"

Running Crane nodded. "Come. You look starved. We have buffalo meat." He set off down the slope without waiting to see whether Weasel Rider followed.

Weasel Rider hurried to catch up. Now he felt safe, he acted insulted that Running Crane had stalked him successfully. "Why does Wolf Eagle watch the stallion while you scout?" he demanded.

"Wolf Eagle has hurt his head. The wound has stolen part of his mind."

"You tell me he is not himself?" Weasel Rider asked, sounding strange.

Running Crane turned to see the older youth's face twisting with anxiety. "He does not remember entering the camp of the Snake People."

At that, Weasel Rider relaxed somewhat. Running Crane lengthened his stride, and Weasel Rider said nothing more before they reached the camp.

They found Wolf Eagle leaning against a tree and chewing imperturbably on a strip of buffalo meat. Showing no surprise on seeing Weasel Rider, the warrior offered him a strip. While Weasel Rider chewed, Wolf Eagle scrutinized him from head to toe. "I do not see your bow," he said, as if nothing else about Weasel Rider mattered.

"I lost my bow," Weasel Rider answered sourly. He had only the remains of the leggings he wore.

"Even your knife and medicine pouch," Wolf Eagle observed.

Weasel Rider shrugged.

"Where are the others?"

Weasel Rider gazed at the treetops. "I do not know. They rode ahead when the Snake herd stampeded."

"You did not ride with them?"

"I did not catch a horse until after they rode away," Weasel Rider said, his head turned.

"You and Red Calf held horses."

Weasel Rider would not meet Wolf Eagle's gaze. "We became separated when the dogs started barking."

"You held horses before the dogs barked?"

"Owl Child gave Red Calf three to hold. I had none."

"You escaped?" Wolf Eagle persisted.

"The horse I caught proved old and slow. I rode with the stampede until after the herd crossed the river. Then I jumped off and hid. The Snake People followed the herd. I have seen none from our party since then."

"And the dogs did not find you," Running Crane offered. Weasel Rider glared angrily, but Running Crane added, "Perhaps they did not find you because they were chasing me."

"We neglect our manners," Wolf Eagle said. "Weasel Rider starves. One strip of meat cannot be enough. He will tell us everything that happened after he has eaten his fill." He rubbed his head in puzzlement. "I recall nothing of the raid, not even dogs barking. Perhaps what he says will help me remember."

Weasel Rider told a disjointed tale filled with inconsistencies. When Wolf Eagle questioned him, his answers became shorter and shorter. Finally Weasel

Rider retreated behind a curtain of surly silence. Running Crane thought perhaps he felt shame about losing his bow or failing to fulfill his boasts that he would capture many fine horses.

After the questions, Wolf Eagle leaned against a tree and slept. Running Crane beckoned Weasel Rider to follow and walked away so their talk would not disturb the injured warrior.

"Wolf Eagle speaks truth about his memory?" Weasel Rider wanted to know.

"Wolf Eagle always speaks truth," Running Crane said. "He does not remember what happened during the raid. When his horse fell and broke a leg, he hurt his head a second time. He remembers falling, and he remembers cutting the horse's throat, but little else. He even lost his war knife."

"He wears the knife," Weasel Rider said, dubious.

"I found it."

"Only someone with an unclear mind would lose his war medicine," Weasel Rider said, his tone hinting of much left unspoken.

"He becomes angry when he cannot move quickly, but I see his strength growing," said Running Crane. "At first, he could not stand. Now he can take several steps before dizziness overcomes him."

Apparently much impressed, Weasel Rider puzzled

about Wolf Eagle's strange malady. He acted heartened, almost pleased, by each reassurance that Wolf Eagle could not remember. "Neither he nor you has seen sign of any others?" he said at last.

"You are the first we have seen," Running Crane told him again.

"Perhaps we alone survived," said Weasel Rider. Satisfaction spread over his face, and he lapsed into thought-filled silence.

CHAPTER EIGHTEEN

Wolf Eagle Remembers

When Weasel Rider approached, the stallion laid back his ears and snapped. Weasel Rider skipped out of the way, then circled as close as he dared, unable to tear his gaze away.

Running Crane could see how much Weasel Rider admired the big horse. Remembering Weasel Rider's empty boasts, he smiled to himself as he secured the travois. When he began to lash Wolf Eagle to the backrest, Weasel Rider looked surprised.

"Sometimes the travois finds a hole," Running Crane explained. "A sharp thump makes Wolf Eagle dizzy. I do not want him to fall off."

Wolf Eagle submitted, scowling. "I feel weak as a newborn. No Blackfoot warrior should have to travel on a travois like butchered meat."

"If a Snake arrow had pierced your thigh, you would not complain," Running Crane told him. They had gone through this grumbling discussion many times.

Weasel Rider set out in the lead, as if he knew the trail. Wolf Eagle needed to correct their course twice before Weasel Rider worked his way to the side so he could follow without appearing to follow. His covert glances stole more and more often toward the stallion. When Running Crane caught him gawking, Weasel Rider looked away and pretended not to notice. Soon he lagged far enough behind that he could watch the great horse without being watched himself.

Running Crane decided Weasel Rider felt disgruntled because he had to walk while another rode. He remembered the feeling very well, having experienced it many times. But now that seemed like a long time ago.

When they reached the next campsite, Wolf Eagle settled himself at the base of a tree and began to eat. "Buffalo is the only proper food for a Blackfoot," he rumbled, satisfied. He made the words sound very different from the way Weasel Rider once said them.

"You had good fortune to find a buffalo carcass fresh enough to butcher," Weasel Rider commented.

"We did not find a buffalo carcass," replied Wolf Eagle. "Running Crane killed a black horn from the back of his buffalo-runner."

"With *his* bow?" Weasel Rider sneered. "He used every arrow twice."

"With *my* bow," Wolf Eagle corrected.

"You acted kindly stringing your bow for him," Weasel Rider attempted.

"He strung the bow himself."

"I had to struggle," said Running Crane, offering Weasel Rider a graceful path of retreat. Somehow he no longer felt the need to prick his former tormentor with words.

"Then the stallion cannot be the spirit horse of the Snake People, although he looks something like that one," Weasel Rider insisted. "And Running Crane had even greater fortune to find a trained buffalo-runner."

"If I am any judge of horses, that is the horse of the Snake People," Wolf Eagle said, and everyone knew his fame as a judge of horses. "I may not remember what happened during our raid, but I can still recognize a horse I have seen before."

Weasel Rider tried again. "So the spirit horse did

run off with the Snake herd, and someone broke him before Running Crane rode him."

"Running Crane walked the horse down alone, and he broke him alone," Wolf Eagle informed him.

"How could that be?" Weasel Rider demanded hotly, as if the very idea reflected calculated insult upon his own horsemanship. "Falls Off can barely ride an aged mare."

"Ask Running Crane," said Wolf Eagle, ignoring Weasel Rider's name-calling. With an owlish expression, he nodded toward Running Crane. "He must tell his own story."

A secret twinkle in the warrior's eye let Running Crane know he intended to put Weasel Rider in his place. They shared the understanding, and Running Crane's spirit soared. For the first time since his father walked the Wolf Trail, a warrior had taken a real interest in him.

Weasel Rider disliked having to ask Running Crane how he caught the stallion, but he burned to know. To find out, he had to swallow his pride. "You found a way to capture the stallion," he mumbled finally, his voice barely audible. "You tamed him."

"The story will take much time to tell," Running Crane replied. "Do you wish to hear?"

Weasel Rider had to accept. Time and again, he sniffed derisively, but Running Crane felt no need to challenge the older boy's rude skepticism. When he told of his escape from the grizzlies, Weasel Rider hooted.

"If the rest of the tale is as true as that," he sneered, "I must find another to tell me what happened."

"Show him your leg," Wolf Eagle ordered.

Running Crane did.

Weasel Rider's eyes grew round as he looked at the scars left by the grizzly's claws. After that, he listened in glum silence, marveling in spite of himself. How could this clumsy Siksika from the far north who knew so little about horses come to have such good fortune? Then he thought he had the answer.

"We made a mistake about the stallion, then," he said. "Surely someone broke this horse before. The Snake People did something to drive it crazy."

"That may be true," Running Crane agreed.

"True or not," Wolf Eagle declared, "that changes nothing. When Hunts-Smoke-Rising and Owl Child first saw the spirit horse, they saw a killer. When I saw the spirit horse, I saw a killer. When Running Crane saw the spirit horse running free on the prairie, he saw that same killer. Running Crane did well to walk the horse down. He did well to tame the horse. You have seen the buffalo hide and that scalp on the travois."

Wolf Eagle stared at Weasel Rider until he answered.

"I see. Where did you find the hide?"

"That hide belonged to the medicine bull that your arrow missed," Wolf Eagle said, contemptuous now. "Running Crane killed that bull with my bow. He needed only two arrows. He rode his buffalo-runner. I saw him."

"Your bow has strong medicine," Weasel Rider retorted, angry to hear so much about Running Crane. "Everyone knows that."

Wolf Eagle arched his brows in surprise at Weasel Rider's compulsive boldness. Weasel Rider would never have dared speak thus had the warrior felt well and strong.

Weasel Rider's angry words cascaded forth unchecked. "Running Crane did something to cause the Snakes to discover us. Let him deny that if he can."

"I do not believe that," Wolf Eagle declared.

"But he brings misfortune. He has no medicine."

"I have medicine," Wolf Eagle declared. "I have strong medicine. When we return to our people, I shall share my medicine with Running Crane."

Weasel Rider spat venomously. "Sharing it with him would insult your medicine. Running Crane does nothing well but the work of women. He will never become a warrior. He would tremble in fear to feed a Snake dog — if he ever saw one."

"Afraid?" Wolf Eagle responded, infuriated by the disrespectful outburst. This insolent boy had the effrontery to tell him he should not share his medicine!

Weasel Rider plunged onward, heedless of the consequences. "Either too afraid, or he would have saved no meat. He would run for help."

"I did save meat," Running Crane exclaimed. "I saved meat even though someone said I need not bother."

"Running Crane did save meat," Wolf Eagle echoed in wonder. "I remember. He did save meat. He did not come running to me for help — but someone did. Someone ran to me pleading for me to save him from a little Snake dog."

Wolf Eagle's gaze drifted upward as memories came tumbling back to him, their release triggered by Weasel Rider's accusations. "Someone ran toward me whining for help," he mused softly. His gaze came back to the present and focused upon Weasel Rider. "Weasel Rider came running toward me whining for help. I remember. I told Weasel Rider to stay with Red Calf and hold horses. I told him to stay away from the spirit horse so the stallion would not alert the Snake People."

Weasel Rider quailed before Wolf Eagle's dark glare.

"A dream spoke to me," he wailed. "The spirit horse came in my dream. He said he could not wait any longer to escape from the Snake camp."

Wolf Eagle could not refute Weasel Rider's claim. A true dream brought a sacred message which one could not ignore except upon the greatest peril. No person would dare deny another's dream, but Wolf Eagle could voice questions.

"Why did you come running to me, then?" he asked. "Did your dream tell you to do that?"

"My dream told me to cut the spirit horse free," Weasel Rider claimed.

"Yet you called out for my protection," Wolf Eagle recalled. "The stallion pursued you and found me. I saw the horse rear. I saw the hooves. . . . My memory ends there, but I remember that much. You woke the Snake People. I feel certain of that."

Wolf Eagle fell silent for a long time as he considered the memories that had just returned to him.

"I had a dream," Weasel Rider repeated.

"If your dream said to cut the spirit horse free," Wolf Eagle said at last, "you had to heed your medicine. But, if your medicine means danger to your own people, you should be the last to accuse another of bringing misfortune."

Weasel Rider humphed as if he felt vindicated, then stalked away. When he returned, he acted as if nothing had happened. He maintained his place in the march all the next day.

When Running Crane caught him gazing at the stallion, Weasel Rider's resentful glare glowed hotter. Even so, Running Crane felt concern for him. Weasel Rider would tell his story, but it would deceive no one. A dream did not excuse cowardice. Weasel Rider would find himself the butt of endless jokes. Running Crane knew how that felt.

When they camped, Wolf Eagle grumbled about his weakness, but he said he felt stronger. Weasel Rider accepted his portion of buffalo meat, then retreated to sulk in silence. Wolf Eagle and Running Crane ignored him.

"We shall reach our people tomorrow," Wolf Eagle said. "Another day, and we might have to eat rabbit again."

"Or I would have to kill another buffalo," Running Crane amended. "I should have butchered the spirit bull."

"You could not know we would have another person to feed." Wolf Eagle assured him. "Besides, we have enough. Tomorrow night we shall feast."

"Do you think any of the others escaped?" Running Crane asked.

"I think most returned," Wolf Eagle answered confidently. "You said Snakes found our war lodge. They would not have searched unless they hunted for our people. Hunts-Smoke-Rising becomes like the smoke he hunts. I sometimes think he can make himself invisible. Owl Child and he look after each other. Beaver-Slaps-Tail-Twice and Small Dog and Otter have grown wise in the ways of the warpath. I grow eager to learn more about what happened."

CHAPTER NINETEEN

Treachery

Shortly after midday, Wolf Eagle called a halt in a grove of cottonwoods beside a brawling river. To the north, their source hidden by a low ridge, thin strands of smoke rose vertically in the still air. Like a stand of gray lodgepoles, they stood tall against the sky until a fitful breeze sprang up to twist them into knots, then blow them to shreds. The rushing torrent flowed too deep to ford, and Running Crane gazed doubtfully at the swirling water.

Wolf Eagle raised his voice to make himself heard over the noise of the cicadas and the river. "We do not need to cross. Anyone who fell into the river here would be swept away and lost forever. I followed this path because the prairie flattens out soon. Our Kainaa will see us from a great distance. I do not wish our arrival to surprise them."

"And you shall find the walking easier?" Running Crane asked.

"Do not mock your elders," Wolf Eagle warned. His smile belied his severe tone. "I shall start walking here. I should not be dragged into camp on a travois like a half-butchered buffalo."

Weasel Rider caught up with them. He had lagged behind all morning, his shoulders bowed as though he carried a great weight. Now, however, he straightened, looking darkly resolute.

Running Crane thought he had probably found a new way to explain his dream, a way which might free him of blame for waking the Snake People. At that moment, he really did not care what Weasel Rider might say. He had Wolf Eagle's respect and the offer of his medicine. He had the spirit horse for a buffalo-runner. What more could he ask — except his own medicine dream?

He turned to Wolf Eagle. "Do you wish to ride?"

Weasel Rider's chin came up, his eyes glittering with evil.

"If I thought I could," Wolf Eagle said, "I would gladly ride. But I feel certain the stallion would carry no one but you. You would have to tie me upon his back and lead him. That would feel worse than walking," he added. He clenched his jaws. "We do not have a great distance to walk."

"Then I shall lead the stallion and walk beside you," Running Crane said. He thought of how the Kainaa would receive Weasel Rider, of how Weasel Rider would become the object of all the ridicule that the boys had once directed at him. Then he thought of how alone he had felt. As much as he disliked Weasel Rider, he would not visit that kind of loneliness upon anyone. "Weasel Rider shall walk with us," he said. "We shall not break up our war party. We left together. Let us return together."

Weasel Rider did not answer, but he joined them, still grim.

Dizziness overcame Wolf Eagle before he could walk to the end of the grove. He persevered, but beads of perspiration sprang from his brow. He grew pale and had to sit despite Running Crane's efforts to steady him.

"I have become an old man," he moaned.

"We have no need for hurry," Running Crane said. "Rest a while."

"I shall scout ahead," Weasel Rider said.

"Do not skulk," Wolf Eagle warned. "If any see you, remember you are Kainaa. You belong here."

Running Crane went to fetch water for Wolf Eagle. When he returned, Weasel Rider had left, and Wolf Eagle's eyes were closed.

The cicadas buzzed. A particularly bold one clung to a sapling close behind Running Crane, vibrating furiously. He watched the insect for a time, but no others answered the rasping love song. When he moved closer, the insect stilled its song and sidled to the back of the sapling. Running Crane turned away, settling himself upon the trunk of a fallen cottonwood to wait for Wolf Eagle to wake, and the lovelorn cicada resumed the lonesome refrain.

Now, at the end of their journey, Running Crane did not think about danger. He enjoyed the sounds of the river, the cicadas, the wind in the trees. He gazed at the magnificent stallion he had caught and tamed. The thought of owning such a horse filled his heart with pride. He looked at the travois — crude work, but sound. He looked at the tawny scalp on the backrest. He had killed a mighty medicine bull from his stallion's back.

The sheath for Wolf Eagle's bear-knife caught his eye — empty. Losing that knife would foreshadow bad fortune indeed. How had the knife fallen out? Running Crane reviewed their journey. When he last saw the knife, Wolf Eagle had been tying a thong around the haft. The knife could not have fallen out by accident. What then? Had Weasel Rider taken the knife? Where was Weasel Rider?

The stallion's head jerked up; he started to prance. Danger! The cicada behind Running Crane stopped buzzing. Danger! An eddy of breeze brought a faint rasp.

Running Crane threw himself forward.

A streak of pain seared down his back, and a dull thud sounded behind him. He whirled to see Wolf Eagle's knife driven deep into the tree trunk where he had been sitting. Weasel Rider was yanking on the haft, trying to free it.

Running Crane had only his short knife. He might outrun Weasel Rider, mount the stallion, and ride away, but only if he left Wolf Eagle behind. He would not leave Wolf Eagle. He had to fight.

He drew his stubby knife. If he could reach Weasel Rider before the war knife came loose from the log . . . Too late.

Weasel Rider gave a final wrench and jerked the knife free. He jumped over the log. "I have had another dream," he snarled. "I am going to kill a Siksika and take the spirit horse of the Snake People for my own. Siksikas know nothing of horses. A Siksika does not deserve such a horse." He leaned forward, ready to spring.

Running Crane's stomach churned, and the adventures he had survived flashed before his eyes. Would his adventures now end? Not without a fight. He might die here — but he would not run.

"Ho," exclaimed Weasel Rider. "The clacking reed pretends he will stand against a Kainaa. You will run, Siksika. I will make you run. This knife carries Wolf Eagle's war medicine. This knife will drink your blood."

Running Crane stood his ground. He had to stay between Weasel Rider and the injured warrior. That would make his fight more difficult. "Remember how Wolf Eagle won the knife," he said. "Wolf Eagle did not *lift* that knife from the sheath of a friend. He took the knife from an enemy in battle. The medicine belongs to him."

Weasel Rider sneered grandly. "That will not save you. I do not need Wolf Eagle's medicine. I have his knife. I am stronger than you. I will kill you anyway."

"If you think you can kill me so easily, why did you try for my back? Did fear guide your skulking? Beware! That knife will bring your death if my knife does not."

Weasel Rider did not expect defiance from Running Crane. His determination faltered for a moment, and a hint of doubt crept into his eyes. Then his expression hardened.

"No Siksika will ever tell tales about me," he said. "I will kill you and Wolf Eagle. I will throw your bodies into the river. No one will ever know the Snake People did not catch you."

He feinted. Running Crane dodged back.

"Afraid, Siksika?" Weasel Rider laughed at him, a vicious, brittle laugh like a flint scraping stone.

Running Crane recovered his position.

Weasel Rider sneered again. "Oh, ho! The puny Siksika imagines he can protect the mighty Kainaa warrior. You have no medicine. Your spirit will never find the Wolf Trail. Remember that as you die."

The spirit of battle that had seized Running Crane when he faced the tawny bull entered him again. He knew Weasel Rider. His knife could not defeat Weasel Rider, but his heart and his words might. If Weasel Rider concerned himself so much with medicine, let him have something to think about.

"I have medicine, strong medicine," Running Crane exclaimed. Suddenly he recognized the truth of his words. "My medicine comes with the wind. I tamed a spirit horse when the wind spoke to me. I killed a great bull. I will kill you."

"You lie," Weasel Rider howled, as if shouting would make the words untrue.

Running Crane's thoughts raced furiously. And then he knew what to say. "The wind circles us. Listen. The wind blew to warn me when you stalked my back. How else did I escape you? Feel the wind."

Weasel Rider hesitated. "Your puny knife can barely butcher rabbits," he shouted. "You have no medicine."

A gust of wind swirled earthward from the treetops to raise a cloud of leaf litter and dust.

Weasel Rider hesitated again.

Running Crane pulled back his lips in a grin he did not feel. This had to work. He had no other chance. If Weasel Rider stopped talking and attacked . . . In his mind, he could hear the words he needed.

"Are you ready to die?" he asked. The wind came over his shoulder, blowing in Weasel Rider's face. "The wind listens to our words. The wind will blow dust in your eyes to blind you. You feel the wind. You know the truth."

A stronger gust spiraled downward, rattling the leaves as it came. Running Crane forced another grin. He waited until the first dust began to rise, then crouched to attack.

Weasel Rider gripped the haft of the war knife until his knuckles turned white and he began to shake.

"The wind is coming for you," Running Crane hissed. "I am coming for you!"

"Aaaaagh!" Weasel Rider's scream rent the air. He meant to shout a war whoop, but the sound came out a strangled shriek of fear. His eyes bulged with dread. The wind blew harder. Weasel Rider felt the strength of Running Crane's medicine, stronger than his own.

"Aaaaagh!" he screamed again.

Running Crane forced a step toward the quaking blusterer, then another. Weasel Rider screamed a third time, threw down the knife, and fled.

CHAPTER TWENTY

The Heart of a Horseman

Wolf Eagle yawned and stretched as if he had slept, but Running Crane realized instantly that the warrior had witnessed the entire fight. Unable to help, he had remained silent, trusting a youth with his life.

"I could do nothing," Wolf Eagle said, mentioning neither Running Crane's bravery nor Weasel Rider's cowardice. "You needed no sounds from me to stir the wind you called. Let us go to the encampment."

Running Crane's heart still gyrated madly, and his breath came in ragged gasps. To steady himself, he picked up Wolf Eagle's bow and tested the string with his fingertips. "I have a quarrel which I shall finish."

"Hunt stray dogs if you choose," Wolf Eagle said, settling himself upon the travois. "For myself, I would rather go to feast with our people. We have journeyed long."

Running Crane put down the bow. Weasel Rider had gone. Let him go. None would miss him. The line of pain down his back reminded him how narrowly he had escaped.

Wolf Eagle eyed the shallow cut and clucked. "Be glad you grew no thicker," he said, holding his fingers a hair's thickness apart. "You came this close to walking the Wolf Trail. The knife cut clean, and the blood will soon stop, but the wound will knit more quickly if you do not draw a bow."

The stallion smelled the blood and shifted uneasily. When Running Crane rubbed the soft nose, speaking encouragement, the stallion whickered and nuzzled him. Running Crane patted the great horse's neck. Watching as Wolf Eagle composed himself for the final leg of their long journey, he felt content. A horse such as this one and a friend such as Wolf Eagle — what more did he need?

"You speak wisely," he agreed. He put the bow away and mounted.

When they neared the last rise, Running Crane reined the stallion to a halt. He could hear dogs barking and a drum. The excited shouts of playing children floated across the distance. "If you will not ride alone, will you ride double with me?" he asked.

"A fine buffalo-runner should not carry double like a common pack horse," Wolf Eagle answered.

"A great warrior should not ride on a travois like a half-butchered carcass," said Running Crane, using the words Wolf Eagle had spoken so many times.

Wolf Eagle grunted. "I will ride double, but you shall ride in front. You captured the spirit horse, and you tamed him. You succeeded alone where a band of Snake People failed. Even if the others returned with horses to divide, we will not count the stallion among them. The stallion belongs to you. Help me mount."

When Wolf Eagle struggled up the leg of the travois, the stallion flicked his ears and started to prance. Running Crane spoke gently and rubbed the horse's neck until he accepted the double burden.

"The stallion trusts you," Wolf Eagle observed. "You should feel pride that a spirit horse trusts you."

Scouts saw them when they topped the rise, and a party of armed warriors raced their horses to meet them. They whooped in greeting when they recognized Wolf Eagle, then sent a boy riding at breakneck speed back to the encampment with the news. Soon another mounted party appeared from the circle of tipis and raced toward them.

"I see Owl Child," Running Crane exclaimed. "And Hunts-Smoke-Rising. The others ride with them."

Moments later the rest who had gone on the raid with Wolf Eagle reined in their horses at a respectful distance. The stallion laid his ears back and shrilled a challenge. Running Crane needed all his skill to keep him under control.

"Have you walked the Wolf Trail?" Small Dog asked. "You ride the spirit horse. Do we see ghosts?"

"Flesh and blood," Wolf Eagle assured him. He wiped a hand across Running Crane's back and showed the blood for all to see. "Running Crane bleeds even now."

The arrival of more whooping riders made talk impossible. Beaver-Slaps-Tail-Twice, Owl Child, Hunts-Smoke-Rising, Small Dog, Otter, and Red Calf escorted Running Crane and Wolf Eagle in triumph back to the encampment.

When they arrived, Running Crane had to slide down immediately to hold the stallion. The great horse laid his ears back and shrilled challenge after challenge. Wolf Eagle managed to dismount without assistance. He nodded solemnly at Running Crane, then winked before his sits-beside-him wife and another helped him to his tipi.

The crowd admired for a long time before they satisfied their eyes and Running Crane could lead the nervous stallion clear. His mother waited.

"You have grown," she told her son by way of greeting, glancing only briefly at the stallion. Despite her unseemly worries before he left, she acted with restraint now, treating him like a warrior. She looked at his bare feet and the tattered, blood-stained remnants of his clothing with a mother's eye and sniffed disparagingly, but Running Crane could feel her pride.

That night, the war party gathered beside the fire in Wolf Eagle's tipi. They raised its sides, and a surging wall of faces crowded close around, straining to hear.

Running Crane sat in the place of honor on Wolf Eagle's left. His mother had made him new leggings, but he wore his buffalo-trampled shirt. She had sewn up the back clucking under her breath with every stitch, but the medicine bull's hoof marks showed clearly.

Wolf Eagle passed a medicine pipe before he began to speak, then told his own story first, as was proper.

When he finished, he turned to Running Crane. "You shall speak," he ordered.

Running Crane looked around the circle of expectant faces. Never before had so many wanted to hear his words. He cleared his throat, but his voice would not come.

"Do not spare your words," Wolf Eagle said. "Words have served you well." He added with a twinkle in his eye, "Begin with the spirit bull. And remember the muskrat who attacked you when we crossed the river."

Running Crane laughed.

He relived hiding from the Snake People's dogs and escaping the grizzlies and walking down the stallion. When he came to finding Wolf Eagle and the medicine bull's second attack, he tried to stop, but Wolf Eagle urged him on. He made no mention of Weasel Rider, but he felt certain Wolf Eagle would tell the others when the time came.

Afterward, other members of the war party related what had happened to them.

"How many horses did you bring back?" Wolf Eagle asked for all to hear, although he already knew.

"Sixty," said Owl Child. "The finest of their herd."

"Snake People tried to retake some," Small Dog put in. "But we found them." He told how the Kainaa drove the raiders off. "They took only a few old packhorses."

"Have you divided the herd?" Wolf Eagle asked.

"We have waited for you to return," Beaver-Slaps-Tail-Twice replied.

"We knew you would," Owl Child added.

The others agreed.

"We have returned," Wolf Eagle said. "We shall divide the horses tomorrow. I shall give of my portion to Running Crane. Without him, I would have walked the Wolf Trail."

"I would give of mine also, if that would grant me knowledge of Running Crane's medicine," said Owl Child.

The listeners gasped, for all knew well the strength of Owl Child's own medicine.

"I would gladly share my medicine," said Running Crane. "If I knew how. But no kindly spirit has taught me sacred songs. I have no symbols of power. I do not yet know how to call upon any spirit to assist me."

Sounds of disagreement arose around the fire.

Then Owl Child drew himself up proudly and spoke. "You do have medicine, Siksika," he said. "Strange medicine, but strong. You showed your medicine when you caught the pointed stick at our war camp. You paid for your catch with blood, but you did not falter. You caught the medicine horse and paid for your capture with blood, but again you did not falter."

"He will learn of his medicine," said Hunts-Smoke-Rising. "I would give of my horses against that day."

All eyes turned toward the silent warrior, and the hearers gasped in amazement at the great length of his speech.

When Running Crane's next turn to speak came, he said, "I shall give of my horses to Red Calf. He taught me much."

Everyone murmured approval. Such generosity from a youth who before this day owned but a single horse!

"Running Crane has proven himself a warrior," Wolf Eagle concluded solemnly. "He has grown too tall for the name of his youth. I now give him a new name worthy of his deeds. From this day I shall call him Talks-with-the-Wind. I believe he shall find in his name greater medicine than he yet understands. Let us speak carefully the name of Talks-with-the-Wind, for his name betokens much. He has much to learn, but he has the heart of a horseman. We shall be honored to count him among us."

Outside the tipi, the stallion whinnied. Talks-with-the-Wind smiled, content.

Spirit Horse takes place in Blackfoot Indian country, now Montana and Alberta, during the 1770s. This was a time of rapid change for the Blackfoot, a period of freedom and glory when they were the most powerful tribe of the northwestern plains.

The Blackfoot People were comprised of three major groups sharing the same language and customs: the Siksika to the north, the Kainaa in the center, and the Northern and Southern Peigans to the south. Individuals frequently moved from band to band. They intermarried and fought common enemies.

During the time this story takes place, Europeans had not begun to invade in large numbers. Metal pots and arrowheads were becoming available, but muskets remained very rare. Making war against their enemies and hunting buffalo were the principle occupations of Blackfoot men.

Horses were becoming widespread on the Great Plains, and they became the measure of Blackfoot wealth. Bands and individual warriors could become "rich" and own a great many horses. With the use of the horse-drawn travois, tipis became larger and personal possessions more numerous. The horse-drawn travois also meant the old and the infirm need not be abandoned when they could no longer walk, and their long memories contributed much to Blackfoot lore and culture.